P9-CLD-269

The Arrival

Even the book morphs!
Flip the pages
and check it out!

Look for other ANIMORPHS® titles by K.A. Applegate:

#1 The Invasion
#2 The Visitor
#3 The Encounter
#4 The Message
#5 The Predator
#6 The Capture
#7 The Stranger
#8 The Alien
#9 The Secret
#10 The Android
#11 The Forgotten
#12 The Reaction
#13 The Change
#14 The Unknown
#15 The Escape
#16 The Warning
#17 The Underground
#18 The Decision
#19 The Departure
#20 The Discovery
#21 The Threat
#22 The Solution
#23 The Pretender
#24 The Suspicion
#25 The Extreme
#26 The Attack
#27 The Exposed
#28 The Experiment
#29 The Sickness
#30 The Reunion
#31 The Conspiracy
#32 The Separation
#33 The Illusion
#34 The Prophecy
#35 The Proposal
#36 The Mutation
#37 The Weakness

<MEGAMORPHS>

#1 The Andalite's Gift
#2 In the Time of Dinosaurs
#3 Elfangor's Secret

the andalite chronicles

The Hork-Bajir Chronicles
Visser

ALTERNAMORPHS

The First Journey

ANIMORPHS®

The Arrival

K.A. Applegate

SCHOLASTIC INC.
New York Toronto London Auckland Sydney
Mexico City New Delhi Hong Kong

The author wishes to thank Kim Morris for her help in preparing this manuscript.

For Michael and Jake

Cover illustration by David B. Mattingly
Art Direction/Design by Karen Hudson

ISBN 0-439-10677-X

12 11 10 9 8 7 6 5 4 3 2 1 0 1 2 3 4 5/0

Printed in the U.S.A.
First Scholastic printing, February 2000

CHAPTER 1

Crumph! Crumph!

The thudding of fists against human flesh is not a pleasant sound. It is particularly sickening when heard through a metal pipe. The sound echoes and is magnified.

"That's enough. Stop it," a human voice commanded. The sound was muffled, vague, indistinct. I was feeling the voice through my six legs, through my antennae.

"But he's told us nothing," a second human argued.

I should not call them humans. They are human-Controllers.

There is a difference.

Human-Controllers are humans whose bodies have become hosts to the Yeerk invaders.

Yeerks! Foulest creatures of the universe. Gray slugs who enter the body through the ear, fit themselves into the human brain, and take over. Mind and body.

Of course, not all hosts are human.

Visser Three, leader of the Yeerk Earth invasion, has an Andalite host.

My name is Aximili-Esgarrouth-Isthill. I am not human. I am Andalite. The only Andalite among the group that calls itself the Animorphs. Four humans. A red-tailed hawk. Me.

We are the resistance. We fight the Yeerk invasion until help from my home planet arrives. Or until we die.

The latter possibility seems ever more likely.

It would be unwise to tell you very much more. The Animorphs and I have many secrets to keep. And I, as an Andalite, have the secret of my own race to keep.

Crumph!

The sound again. Had we not been on the pipe we would not have heard it. Roaches feel vibrations. The pipe carried those vibrations directly to us.

We were making our way up a corroded, rusty metal pipe within the interior wall of a two-story office building. Our mission, to rescue our friend and collaborator, Mr. King. We had all seen the front page article on The Sharing, the Yeerk front organization. We had been suspicious that the paper had become yet another Yeerk-run organization. Mr. King had thought it safe to break into the offices of *The Chronicle* and examine their computer data, find the truth.

Apparently that was a mistake.

"Talk!" human-Controller Two shouted. "What are you doing here? Who are you? Why are you snooping?"

Crumph!

"I said stop it!" human-Controller One repeated angrily. "If you kill him, Visser Three will execute us for wasting a potential host body."

There was a long pause before human-Controller Two spoke again. "Visser Three will execute us for incompetence if he finds out we couldn't beat the truth out of a mere human. Let's kill him and incinerate the body. Visser Three will never learn that we failed."

"Visser Three will wonder why we did not simply infest him and learn the truth."

"I tell you there is something wrong with this human. I tried to enter the ear canal, but it's blocked in some way. You don't believe me, you try it!"

<Ax? What happens if they hit the Chee with a Dracon beam? Can they fry him?> Prince Jake

asked me in the thought-speak language we use while in morph.

<I am assuming that it would depend on the amount of power used. A low setting might only disturb the Chee's holographically projected body. It would reveal the android beneath. But a full-power setting could very possibly destroy Mr. King entirely. Which would be worse from our own narrow perspective? It is an interesting question.>

<Thanks, Spock,> Marco said, using the human tone I've come to recognize as sarcasm. <Sure you're not a Vulcan?>

<Vulcans are fictional creatures,> I replied. <And not a particularly convincing creation. Variations among real alien species tend to involve more than cosmetic variations in ear formation and eyebrow alignment. As I believe you may have noticed.>

Marco said, <Hey! Who just crawled over my back?>

<Sorry,> Cassie said. <Lousy visibility.>

The sound of a new blow came echoing through the pipe again. "Talk! Talk or we'll kill you!"

We were inside the wall. To one side, the torture. On the other side? We would have to find out.

Prince Jake's voice was sharp and urgent. <Follow me and get ready to morph.>

<Why doesn't Mr. King just walk out of there and save us a whole lot of trouble?> Marco asked.

<What's the problem, Marco, missing the *Rugrats* marathon?> That was Rachel. Rachel never found reason to resist action.

For my own part I sympathized with Marco. The Chee were frustrating. Very useful allies. But also liabilities. My human friends have a certain sentimental sympathy for the pacifism of the Chee. I do not.

<Rachel, have I mentioned that I consider you the most attractive cockroach around? Psychotic, yet with a certain cockroach style.>

Rachel laughed. <Anyway, there's two of them and five of us. So don't wet yourself.>

<We're here,> Prince Jake announced.

<Any idea where "here" is?> Cassie inquired.

<Here's where there's an eighth of an inch crack,> Prince Jake explained. <That's good enough for me.>

Prince Jake navigated a bend in the pipe and crossed to the wall itself. Above him was a tiny thread of light. I followed.

Prince Jake flattened his body. Disappeared between two boards.

I did the same.

We emerged into the light. I fought the instinct to panic and retreat back into the baseboard. I waved my antennae, checking for danger.

<All clear,> Prince Jake announced, although his roach senses were no better than mine. He had to be making an educated guess. <Demorph!>

<Let's rock and roll,> Rachel said.

Rock and roll is a type of human music. Its relevance to the battle before us was a mystery to me.

CHAPTER 2

Morphing is an odd and disturbing process. It is never the same twice. The last time I came out of cockroach morph, my hind legs were the first portions of my Andalite anatomy to emerge.

This time, it was my eyes.

The two that are on stalks. Not the ones on my face. I had no face at the moment so eyes would have been quite out of place.

I felt the nub of both stalks pushing out through my hard, insect exoskeleton. My head split with an audible crack.

It was not painful. At least not in the conventional sense. But there was a sense that it *should* hurt. Therefore while there is no actual pain,

there is the anticipation of pain. Which, in its own way, is quite painful.

My two eye stalks emerged and I was able to see the others with far more clarity than the roach's dim senses allowed.

Marco. Rachel. Cassie. And Prince Jake. All demorphing from roach to human. Neither transition, roach to Andalite or roach to human, is attractive to watch. I try to be sensible about such things but it is simply disturbing to watch human flesh grow out of a roach's hard, caramel-colored exoskeleton. The melting of enlarged roach mouthparts to re-form as human mouthparts is particularly unsettling. Possibly because for an Andalite all mouths seem alien.

We were in a room filled with what appeared to be filing cabinets. There were newspapers piled high in stacks. The sound of torture came from the other side of the wall.

<Still clear outside here,> Tobias reported. He sounded bored. <Just watching the moon go by overhead.>

Tobias is a *nothlit*, a person who overstays the two-hour limit and becomes trapped in morph. He has, in fact, reacquired his power to morph and could, should he choose to do so, resume human form permanently. Assuming he would be willing to become a sort of human *nothlit*, trapped forever in his original form, never able to morph again.

He has chosen to remain a red-tailed hawk. He usually provides air surveillance for us during a mission.

Prince Jake looked at the others. And then at me. "Ax, you go in as yourself. Everybody else, battle morphs. We're doing this fast. And we're doing it right."

We heard the door to the next office open and close.

"I brought in three Dracon beams," human-Controller Two said. "Enough to reduce him to a little pile of ash."

Prince Jake began the tiger morph. His eyeteeth grew, surging forward like plunging daggers. Two sharp tiger ears sprouted from his hair before his own human ears disappeared, creating a very odd appearance.

His forearms bent at an odd angle, growing shorter and sprouting orange-and-black fur.

The others were right behind him. Or, in Cassie's case, ahead of him. She is quite talented at morphing. I was soon in the company of a tiger, a wolf, a grizzly bear, and a gorilla.

If someday an Andalite reads this and wonders what these animals represent, I should point out that the animals of Earth are often very pow-

erful, capable of doing tremendous damage with a combination of claws, teeth, lightning reflexes, and highly acute senses. Among the animals of Earth, these four, each with its own strengths and weaknesses, formed a powerful force.

For human readers I should explain that my own Andalite body is of course sufficient for battle situations. I have four eyes, four legs, two arms, and a tail blade that can slice a human in half with one swipe.

Well, perhaps two swipes. I may perhaps have a tendency to overstate my capabilities.

<They're right on the other side of that wall,> Cassie said. Her wolf senses could pinpoint our targets within a few feet one way or the other.

<Too bad there's no door,> Prince Jake said. <Rachel? Marco? Ax? Make a door.>

Rachel stood. Eight hundred pounds of loose, shaggy brown fur over massive muscle and bone.

KABOOM!

Rachel slammed into the wall.

The flimsy drywall cracked from baseboard to ceiling in several places.

"What the . . . ?" Before the human-Controller on the other side of the wall could finish his cry . . .

SNAP!

Marco grabbed the cracked wallboard and ripped it back.

Fwapp! Fwapp!

I whipped my tail over my head and sliced the bent Sheetrock so that it fell away with a clatter and a puff of dust.

Cassie was through the gap in a flash of gray fur, teeth bared. Jake was right behind her.

"Andalites!" the two human-Controllers screamed.

The Yeerks believe we are all Andalites. Actually there was just the one Andalite. Me.

I felt that would be enough.

CHAPTER 3

It was a small room. Badly lit. One wall was formed of reinforced glass and beyond that glass a dark office.

I should have worried about that. We all should have. But our attention was drawn to what appeared to be a badly beaten human, barely holding onto consciousness, slumped on a chair. His arms were bound behind his back with metal chains called handcuffs. His ankles were likewise affixed to the legs of the chair.

One of the human-Controllers was drawing a gun. He took aim at Cassie. Cassie's teeth found his arm in midair. The man screamed.

BLAM! His shot went wild.

BLAM! BLAM!

The second Controller fired two shots at Rachel. One missed. The other nicked her shoulder. It was badly aimed. Most likely because Marco was shaking him like a rag doll.

Fwapp! Fwapp!

I hit each of the Controllers with the flat of my tail. Both fell unconscious.

The seemingly near-dead Mr. King sat up, suddenly whole, healthy, and unscarred, calmly snapped the handcuffs, and said, "Thanks for coming to get me."

<Keep up the pretense,> I warned. <There may be others of the enemy around.>

"Ah, yes." The wounds, the blood all reappeared instantly. He let out a very convincing groan and slumped.

Marco dropped the human-Controller and picked up Mr. King. <Okay! Let's get out of here.>

Rachel swung her arms from her enormous shoulders, impatient. <That was too easy,> she complained. <Maybe . . .>

<Uh-oh!> Marco said.

Something was moving beyond the reinforced glass. Several somethings. Hork-Bajir! And one shape that was terribly familiar.

Visser Three!

<It's a trap!> Prince Jake shouted.

I stared at the heavily muscled adult Andalite

body. At the tail blade that could kill with one swipe. Looked with hatred at the only Andalite-Controller in the galaxy.

Visser Three had no right to that body. No right to the eyes. The brain. The strength. The speed. No right to the morphing power.

Visser Three is an evil thing. A Yeerk slug within the brain of an Andalite who had once been called Alloran-Semitur-Corrass.

Alloran's was a hideous fate. He was still alive. His mind and memories intact. He was a slave of his own enemy. And he knew the depths of his own powerlessness.

Crrrraaassshhh!

The glass partition fell in splinters.

The visser leaped. Straight for me.

Fwapp!

I blocked the blow. Barely. He was fast, very strong. Stronger than me.

But I was not alone.

"ROOAARRRR!" The tiger's roar shook the light fixtures! Their fluorescent glow flickered!

Jake bounded over three desks and landed, claws extended, on the visser's back.

His claws raked deep and drew blood.

Tseeew! Tseeew!

The Hork-Bajir were firing. All that saved us was the care the Hork-Bajir had to take not to hit their master.

Prince Jake rolled off the visser and onto the floor. His fur burned and smoked where a Dracon beam had penetrated the muscled shoulder.

<To the door!> Prince Jake yelled.

Marco yanked it open.

An armed Hork-Bajir stood in the doorway. More behind him. How many? Too many.

We were blocked in two directions. The only way out was the hole we had made to get in.

No time to think. The visser was on me.

Fwapp!

He struck. I felt his blade bite. Felt my left front leg go numb from the blow.

Fwapp!

I blocked, but he knocked my tail, whipping back. Too strong! I was as fast, but he had power I couldn't match.

Fwapp!

I felt the wind of the blow on my exposed neck.

I drew back and then made a lunatic feint. It threw him off balance.

Small victory. And temporary.

The visser ducked his upper body, clearing the firing line, and roared, <Fire!>

<Down!> I yelled.

Tseeew! Tseeew!

Beams singed the fur down both sides of my back. The wall behind me was all burning wall-

board and wood, half-incinerated by the Dracon beams.

<Rachel! Get the Chee out!> Prince Jake ordered.

Tseeew! Tseeew!

<Ahh!> Jake cried. One of his legs was simply gone, a sizzling, bleeding stump.

<Marco! On me!> Rachel yelled. She charged toward the exit door, straight into the nearest Hork-Bajir blocking our path. The Hork-Bajir folded, crumpled. Marco was right behind Rachel with the Chee on his shoulder.

Tseeew! Tseeew!

A hole the size of a fist burned through Rachel. But the grizzly is not easily stopped.

<Out the way we came in!> Rachel yelled.

They pushed back through our own doorway. Into the file room.

<The hallway over here is clear,> Rachel yelled. <Come on!>

<Okay, bail out!> Jake ordered.

But before I could run, a sound. My stalk eyes swung upward in response to the noise. Ceiling panels were being pulled up as if they were trapdoors.

Hork-Bajir began to drop like hailstones.

CHAPTER 4

<Marco! Take care of Mr. King!> Prince Jake ordered. <Rachel! Hang back with us. Tobias! If you're still out there, get ready to cover Marco!>

We plowed down the hallway, staggering, bleeding, scared. Not fast enough. The Hork-Bajir were rushing up behind us, slashing, cutting into muscle and sinew.

I killed one with a lucky swipe of my tail. He fell and tripped one of his brothers. The two of them sprawled, delaying the rush by a split second.

Down a dark hallway, walls all around, hemming us in, a tunnel, and with Hork-Bajir roaring after us. If they were ahead of us as well . . .

Stairwell leading down. Freight elevator just

ahead. Hallway took a turn just past the elevator. Which way? Prince Jake's decision, but Prince Jake was weakening, stumbling. How much longer could he keep going on three legs?

I wasn't much better off. Bleeding. Staggering. Hurt.

"Sssree! Sssree!"

A frenzy of squealing from below!

Taxxons!

Enormous voracious centipedes. Drawn by the carnage. Forcing their way up the narrow stairwell. Scrambling over the fallen Hork-Bajir, tearing limbs and pieces of flesh from their still-breathing bodies.

Visser Three stepped into the hallway directly ahead. How? Some back way. We were surrounded.

<The elevator,> Prince Jake gasped.

I slammed the button, willing it to come quickly.

Where was Marco? He had gone down the hallway where the visser now appeared. Had he escaped? Or was he already a prisoner?

<I knew a front-page article on The Sharing would bring the Andalite bandits from undercover,> Visser Three sneered. To his troops he said, <I don't want them dead. Lowest power setting. Aim carefully.>

The Hork-Bajir lifted their Dracon beams.

My chest was tight with panic. I could hardly breathe.

My hearts ached for my parents. They had lost one son on this distant planet. I feared they would soon lose a second.

DING!

The doors to the freight elevator opened. The Hork-Bajir wavered, distracted.

<DOWN!> Jake roared.

<FIRE!>

Tseeewww! Tseeewww! Tseeewww!

Dracon beams burned. Inches above us.

And now . . .

Tseeew! Tseeew!

Shredder fire! The sound, so like a Dracon beam, was different enough for any Andalite *aristh* to recognize.

Tseeew! Tseeew!

Shredder fire, point-blank at the wall of tight-packed Hork-Bajir.

<More Andalites?!> Visser Three yelled, his thought-speak voice torn between outrage, fear, and simple disbelief.

Four Andalites jumped from the elevator like bucks clearing a fence. They were everywhere at once. Firing. Whipping their tail blades with deadly precision.

They were magnificent.

I fought beside a young female.

She had impeccable timing. She was dangerous. She was beautiful.

CRASH!

The hallway wall collapsed and the battle spilled back into the interior office space of the building.

The female kept up a steady stream of fire as we forced back the Hork-Bajir line.

Windows shattered. Desks splintered. Plaster, tangles of wire, and debris poured from the ceiling.

The Yeerks were losing.

Suddenly, the shrill sound of police sirens penetrated the noise of battle.

<Hey, cops are on their way,> Tobias announced. <Get out!>

<Did Marco make it out?> Prince Jake demanded, unwilling to run till he was sure we were all safe.

<Yeah. Jumped out of a window and the Chee threw up a hologram, made it look like they were a parked car.>

<Visser,> Prince Jake snapped. <Maybe those cops are your people, but maybe not. Walk away and you live, for now.>

The visser did not deign to respond. He slammed his way past a Taxxon, leaving the creature oozing goo from a deep gash.

The battle was over.

Shell-shocked Hork-Bajir began gathering up their dead. Taxxons waddled back down the stairwell, dragging what meat they could take away with them, to disappear into some secret basement hiding place.

Then, through a cloud of plaster dust, I saw one of the Andalite warriors jump over the body of a fallen Hork-Bajir and land face-to-face with Visser Three.

Of course! These Andalites were not under Prince Jake's orders.

The Andalite lifted his shredder. It would be a point-blank killing.

I felt a surge of hot joy in my heart.

Visser Three looked at the Andalite. <Arbat!>

The Andalite's eyes flickered and his finger hesitated on the shredder.

Fwapp!

With the flat of his tail blade, the visser smacked the weapon from his assailant's hand.

<You never could see that one coming, could you, Arbat?> Visser Three laughed. <That's what comes of thinking too much and tail fighting too little.>

The one he had called Arbat let out an Andalite curse.

Visser Three leaped to safety behind a phalanx of Hork-Bajir.

Prince Jake said, <I don't know who you guys are, but first: Thanks. Second: Get out of here. The cops get in on this and we'll have a massacre of innocent policemen.>

<Withdraw. Now!> one of the Andalites commanded.

<Everybody out!> Prince Jake ordered.

<Wait!> I cried as the Andalites galloped down what was left of the hall. <Who are you? Where can I find you?>

The female turned. <I am Estrid-Corill-Darrath. Do not worry. We will find you, Aximili-Esgarrouth-Isthill.>

CHAPTER 5

An hour later, we were in Cassie's barn.

Cassie's family runs the Wildlife Rehabilitation Clinic. At any given time, the clinic houses several dozen wounded or ill creatures. Often exotics.

There are also squirrels, rabbits, pigeons, and grackles. Common creatures that come and go, drawn by the seeds and oats that lie scattered in and around the barn.

"No doubt about it," Marco said, waving a copy of *The Chronicle*. "A propaganda mill for Yeerks. Part three in a five-part series on The Sharing."

The Sharing exists to recruit human hosts,

willing and unwilling. It poses as an innocuous family-oriented group.

For every Yeerk that has a host body, there are thousands of Yeerks that do not. They live in a dank pool where they feed on Kandrona rays. And wait.

They wait for host bodies.

They would not wait much longer.

<It seems obvious that the Andalite fleet has arrived,> I said. <The Yeerk invasion will soon cease to be a problem.>

"Not so fast, Ax-man," Marco warned.

<How can we lose when even our females fight like trained warriors!> I heard the old Andalite vainglory in my voice. I thought I had outgrown the impulse to boast. But the thrill of fighting side by side with another Andalite had reawakened all the pride of my people.

For the first time since I'd found myself stranded on Earth, I felt that the future might be hopeful.

So I did not understand the look of wariness and pity transmitted from face-to-face.

Cassie. To Rachel. To Prince Jake. To Tobias. To Marco.

Marco spoke. "If I've learned one thing, it's this: It may walk like an Andalite. It may talk like an Andalite. But that don't mean it is an Andalite."

"He's right, Ax." Cassie held a defanged pit viper she had found abandoned in the schoolyard. Gently she pried it from her arm and placed it in a large tub beneath a heat lamp.

"We know it's hard for you, and that you're lonely a lot of the time," Cassie continued. "But . . ."

"But we have to be realistic," Marco finished. "This might be the fleet. Or it might be some fresh hell."

Prince Jake crossed his arms. "How do we know these new Andalites aren't Yeerks with Andalite host bodies?"

<Right,> Tobias agreed. <Maybe a sub-visser and his posse looking to leapfrog to the top by taking out Visser Three.>

<Impossible!> I protested.

"In a world where slugs can take over entire civilizations, anything is possible," Marco reminded me.

<The female knew my name. The only way she could know that is via the message I transmitted to the home planet, or through the forces we encountered on Leera.>

"Funny you should mention Leera," Marco said. He did not say anything more. He did not have to. There, for the first time in my life, I had learned that even an Andalite may be a traitor.

<These warriors are true Andalites,> I in-

sisted. <I know this. When I fought beside the female, I felt a sense of connection unlike anything I have felt before.>

Another look passed from face to face. This time, it appeared to be one of amusement.

"Ax," Cassie said. "I think you have what is commonly known as a crush."

<A what?>

"A feeling that makes it hard for you to see the truth, if the truth is unpleasant," she explained.

"Yeah, you know, like the way Cassie can't see that Jake is really just a pinhead," Marco said.

Prince Jake threw a horse comb at Marco that Marco dodged. Marco and Prince Jake are best friends. This sort of behavior appears to be typical of male friendships.

"Until we figure these guys out, let's just hang loose," Prince Jake said.

"Yeah. Like maybe not change our minds about who is in charge and who isn't," Rachel said bluntly.

I felt myself flush. In the Leera incident I had changed my allegiance from Prince Jake to the Andalite officer who betrayed us.

I was still ashamed of this. But I had sworn never to abandon my prince again. Unless it was at his command.

Shame was quickly replaced by anger.

<Do you doubt my loyalty?> I demanded.

"No, I don't," Prince Jake said firmly. And with a sharp look at Rachel he added, "Neither does Rachel. I just don't want you to do anything without talking it over with us first. Okay?"

<I am a true Andalite warrior,> I said angrily. <And a true warrior never reneges on his oath to his prince.>

I left the barn and galloped until both my hearts were pounding. I was angry, but that emotion cooled quickly enough. The emotion that replaced it did not cool.

She was beautiful.

She was *so* beautiful.

CHAPTER 6

KEEERRRACCKKKK!

I leaped out of range before the tree limb could fall on me. The limb I had severed with one blow of my tail.

<Good shot!> Tobias circled downward, landing in the tree.

Tobias is interesting. A *nothlit*, but now an almost voluntary one. He has lost his human life, but not his human friends. He belongs. But at the same time, he does not belong.

Like me.

Perhaps that is why he is my true *shorm*. What humans would call a "best friend." Or "soul mate." That and the fact that my brother was Tobias's father.

I assumed the attack position again.

<Would you mind not doing that while I'm sitting here?> Tobias asked.

<They said they would find me. I may be called upon to fight at any moment. I must be ready. I must practice.>

Even though I am only an *aristh* — what humans would call a cadet — in the Andalite military, I had undergone rigorous training at the academy. Tail fighting is a sport, an art, and a deadly combat skill.

I had a feeling that I was about to be tested. I did not want to disgrace myself.

<Okay. But you know, it also wouldn't hurt to take a look around town. See if there's any sign of Andalite troop presence. You know, maybe a couple dozen of your folks down at the mall. Besides, I found twenty bucks this morning. Which sounds like a visit to the food court to me.>

<Cinnabon?>

<Cinnabon for you. Me, I'm a taco kind of guy. When I'm not enjoying fresh mouse.>

Cinnamon buns!

I paused. I am extremely fond of cinnamon buns. I am so fond of them, it is hard for me to restrain my joy in eating them.

I have now had much practice eating cinnamon buns. But from time to time, I still have dif-

ficulty containing my enthusiasm for the taste sensations that come from these tasty treats.

This is one of the things I must explain to my people: the incredible joys of acquiring human morphs and using the mouth to ingest intensely flavored items.

I began to morph a northern harrier. The blue-and-tan fur of my body began to grow longer and shingle. Layer upon layer of feathers appeared upon my shrinking body.

<I take it that means yes — especially since I've already hidden our outer clothing on the mall roof,> Tobias said.

We flew over the main part of town. Together. But not close. If Tobias and I were seen flying in tandem, it might attract attention. Yeerk attention.

Once we had landed safely on the mall roof, Tobias began morphing to human.

The sharp angles of his scowling hawk head blurred and rounded out. Flesh appeared on his face first. It swirled and rippled like dough as it arranged itself into human eyes, a human nose, and a human brow.

His bird legs grew enormously long until what began to protrude was no longer bird leg, but bone. The bone formed a femur, a patella, and a tibia. Claws became toe bones.

Flesh poured down the bones like liquid and molded thighs, calves, and feet.

I concentrated. I would have to demorph to Andalite before morphing to human.

Though we have agreed that it is immoral to acquire the DNA of sentient creatures, we also have agreed upon exceptions now and then. I acquired a bit of DNA from Jake, Marco, Cassie, and Rachel. Thus, when I am human, I vaguely resemble all of them, but duplicate no one.

It is a moral compromise.

We have all learned to make them.

The question was how I could make such opportunities available to my fellow Andalites once they landed and defeated the Yeerks.

"Come on," Tobias said as soon as I had morphed from Andalite to human and was properly dressed in my artificial skins. "Let's hit the 'Bon and the Taco Bell."

I followed Tobias toward the small stairwell off the roof used by workmen. Through that door and down two flights of stairs was a door that led into the mall.

We heard the commotion the moment we entered the first floor. It was coming from the food court.

"Beanzuh! Beanzuh! Zuh!" I heard a girl shout.

"Somebody get security!" a woman yelled.

"What's going on?" someone else asked.

"Some girl went berserk in the food court," another person answered. "Eating everything in sight and yelling like a lunatic."

Tobias raised an eyebrow. "Which answers the question of whether the Andalites have landed."

We ran.

CHAPTER 7

"Beanzuh! Jelly beanzuh! Beanzuh! Zuh! Zuh!"

We forced our way through the crowd that had gathered around the food court.

A girl around Cassie's age sat crouched in front of bins of blue, green, yellow, red, and black jelly beans at the Candy Land store. She wore a Burger King tunic and slacks. Backward.

A harassed-looking young woman was trying to persuade her to get away from the bin.

"So sweet. So delicious!" The girl was almost weeping with joy. "The taste . . . overwhelming!"

"Well. This is not good," Tobias said. "Your little friend Estrid?"

"I believe that is likely."

Estrid ignored the Candy Land lady. She crammed more bright pellets into her mouth, rolled her eyes, seemed to be transported by pleasure.

A mall security guard moved toward her. "Okay. Let's go."

Tobias hurried forward and put his hand on the guard's arm. "No wait! She's my sister. She's having a bad reaction to her medication."

"The green are the best!" Estrid said.

The guard looked hard at Tobias. As if he weren't sure whether or not Tobias was telling the truth. "She's on drugs?"

"It's a seizure thing. She was dropped on her head when she was a baby."

"No, the blue! A blue that saturates the very soul with pleasure!"

"Then we should call an ambulance," said the Candy Land lady.

"I like the red ones," a kid in the crowd called out.

"It's happened before," Tobias said. "We know what to do. She calms down . . ."

"Yes! Red! Red-duh!"

". . . Eventually. We have some other medicine at home. If we can just take her with us, everything will be fine."

We both moved toward the shrieking girl.

"But . . ." the security guard said.

"We're fine," Tobias insisted. "Fine. Come on, sis. Let's go home." Tobias took one arm and I took the other.

Estrid looked at each of us, and then let out a horrible, ear-piercing scream. "Nooooo! Bean-zuh!"

"Now, sis," Tobias soothed. "Don't make a scene."

"Sssssseeene. Sssseeeeenuh. Nuh. Nuh. Nuh."

While she was momentarily diverted by the novel sounds her mouth could make, I leaned close and whispered, "It is I, Aximili. You are having a reaction to mouth-pleasures. It will be fine. Come with us and be quiet."

On our way to the door we used to access the mall, I saw a girl inside the doorway of Express. She was examining some artificial skins.

And she was an exact replica of the girl we were half-carrying, half-dragging. Her long hair was red and very wavy. Her eyes were deep blue. And her face was covered with cinnamon-colored freckles.

Cinnamon. Delicious.

"Hey!" a male voice shouted behind us. "What are you doing with my sister?"

Tobias turned. "Holy . . . come on!"

In order to look behind in human morph it is necessary to turn one's head. A dizzying action on only two legs.

I did so and understood the cause of Tobias's alarm.

A very large young man and four of his companions were chasing us.

"She must have morphed his sister. He thinks we're abducting her! Great," Tobias wheezed. "Haul buns."

"Bunzzzzz," I repeated, unable to resist the impulse. "Zuh. Zuh. Zuh."

"Please, Ax," Tobias yelled, breaking into a run. "Not now!"

CHAPTER 8

We escaped from the mall. It was not our most challenging escape.

Estrid morphed to *kafit* bird and flew away. But not before I had arranged for a meeting with her superior. We needed to know what was happening with the Andalite invasion force.

Or, at very least, we had to warn them about the dangers of morphing humans.

A few hours later I was in the air, in harrier morph.

<How much further?> Prince Jake asked.

<If the directions are accurate, less than a mile. There is a fence ahead.>

Prince Jake was on the ground. Traveling in wolf morph. It would have been unwise for me to

travel long distances through the woods in my own true body. I live in some fear that human hunters might see me and shoot me as a deer. Shooting deer is a human sport. Human hunters are apparently unaware of the fact that deer are harmless herbivores.

In the distance ahead, beyond the fence, I could see thick trees around a shallow pond. The scene fit her description.

Estrid had refused to guide me to the Andalite ship. She was not authorized to reveal its location. Commendable caution. But she had agreed to arrange a meeting with her commander in this spot.

Estrid was waiting at the edge of the thicket.

How odd that the sight of one of my own people should seem so strange. It was almost disturbing, somehow. It made me feel lonely, which made no sense. Why should the sight of this single, lovely female make me feel lonely?

I flew a few hundred yards ahead of Jake and landed on the ground in front of her. I demorphed quickly. If this was all somehow a Yeerk ambush, then my presence would trigger the attack. Better me than my prince.

I stood, awkward. Waiting. No Dracon beams. No Hork-Bajir. No Taxxons. No ambush.

<Welcome, Aximili,> Estrid said. <My commander is eager to meet you.>

<Where is he?>

<Near. He fears a trap.>

Before I could respond, I saw her main eyes widen. One stalk eye whipped around. Jake had approached and begun to demorph.

Estrid glared angrily. <I told you to come alone,> she said.

<And I told him not to,> Prince Jake said in thought-speak just as he completed his demorph.

<But he is human!> Estrid exclaimed. <And with the power to morph! How can this be? Wait, were those humans in the battle where we met? Morph-capable humans?>

"I'll discuss that with your commander," Jake said calmly.

<This human is Jake. He is my prince,> I explained.

Estrid looked as if she might laugh. To an Andalite the notion of an alien as a prince was humorous.

But she restrained herself.

<I am honored to meet you, Jake.>

"Likewise."

Then Estrid put a hand on my arm and thought-spoke privately to me. My hearts fluttered at the touch.

<May I ask you a favor? My experimentation with human morph was unauthorized. Will you refrain from mentioning it to my commander?>

For a moment, I was too stunned to answer. Such a breach of discipline! Perhaps females were allowed more latitude and thus felt free to take more liberties.

I did not know. But I could see no harm in protecting her from what might be a harsh punishment.

<I will say nothing,> I promised.

We moved carefully through the dense trees until we reached the banks of the pond. Three Andalite warriors stood tense and watchful.

I said nothing. *Arisths* do not speak until spoken to.

Most *arisths.*

<This is Aximili-Esgarrouth-Isthill,> Estrid said. <These Andalite warriors are Commander Gonrod-Isfall-Sonilli, Intelligence Advisor Arbat-Elivat-Estoni, and Aloth-Attamil-Gahar.>

I saw Commander Gonrod's face tense at her forwardness. But he did not reprimand her. Arbat's eyes smiled slyly.

<And this alien?> Commander Gonrod demanded.

<This is Jake. My prince.>

Gonrod snorted. <Your prince? You insult the highest ranking Andalite within light-years by announcing your allegiance to a human child?>

Prince Jake did not react to the insult. But he

did react to Gonrod's careless words. "Your rank is commander and you're the highest ranking Andalite commander within light-years?" He looked at me, questioning.

I was almost too disappointed to respond. I did not abandon hope. But my optimism was sharply reduced. I could only confirm what Prince Jake suspected. <Commander is a rank most often held by an Andalite in command of a single ship. A single small ship.>

"I see."

<There goes our plan to bluff the enemy into thinking they are outnumbered.> Aloth let out a crack of laughter. Highly insubordinate.

<Silence!> Gonrod looked only at me. He refused to acknowledge Prince Jake. <*Aristh* Aximili, inform this human that we are not prepared to discuss strategic matters with him.>

<Commander Gonrod, Prince Jake is the leader of the human resistance on Earth.>

<Really? And how many warriors does he lead?> Commander Gonrod asked me.

"Not enough," Prince Jake said bluntly.

<No. Not enough. But morph-capable. I was briefed before we began this mission.> Gonrod reluctantly addressed Prince Jake. <I know you were involved in the war on Leera. I also know that an entire ship full of Andalite warriors died

and that you and your humans survived. Now, I asked, human, how many warriors do you command?>

<Those warriors on Leera died because of —> I began, but Prince Jake silenced me with a raised hand.

"We were on Leera. Let's leave it at that. I don't want to bring up anything embarrassing. No point. But you'll understand if I say that I'm not prepared to discuss my forces with you. Not yet."

<You, a human, do not trust an Andalite commander?!> Gonrod cried.

Aloth spoke. Mockingly. <Perhaps the human is not aware that Andalites are known throughout the galaxy for their integrity.>

<*Silence!*> Gonrod roared again.

<Perhaps we should proceed by outlining our common goals,> I suggested diplomatically.

"Perhaps we should begin by finding out exactly what we can count on in terms of Andalite support," Jake countered, staring fixedly at Gonrod.

<Support?> Gonrod snorted again. <You consider us support? Are all humans as ignorant and arrogant as you, man-child?> Gonrod began to pace. <You are an untrained human child, playing at war. We are highly trained warriors. You

and your band, whoever they may be, will cease to fight. *That* is an order.>

"I don't take orders," Prince Jake snapped. "I give them. And now, this meeting is over." He turned and began to walk away.

<*Aristh* Aximili!> Gonrod shouted. <Stay where you are.>

<Commander Gonrod. I respectfully remind you that an Andalite's allegiance is to his prince.>

<You are disobeying a direct order.>

I followed Prince Jake.

<Aloth! Arbat!> Gonrod shouted. <Shredders on lowest setting. Fire on *Aristh* Aximili.>

CHAPTER 9

<Unfortunately, Commander Gonrod, I am being prevented from using my weapon,> Arbat answered. <I believe Aloth is similarly situated.>

Aloth had apparently not noticed. Now he looked down in horror. A pit viper wound itself around his right foreleg. Cassie, of course. And a cobra reared up just between Arbat's legs. Marco.

Estrid took a step forward and reached for her own shredder.

Fwapp!

I brought my tail blade to a quivering halt millimeters from her throat. Her eyes blazed in anger.

"Andalites are very fast," Prince Jake said.

"Those snakes are faster. One move from your boys and they will die."

Gonrod said nothing. He seemed at a loss. It was shocking to see in an Andalite commander.

But Arbat was so calm as to seem almost bored. <So, you've set a trap for us. Very clever. Now what?>

Prince Jake seemed uncertain whether to continue addressing Gonrod or Arbat. "Now we stop playing games. You're not the Andalite fleet. And I'm not going to snap a salute and say 'yes, sir!' We deal as equals. Which, to be honest, is generous of us under the circumstances."

Arbat half-closed his eyes in a smile. <What do you say, Commander Gonrod? As the Intelligence expert I'd have to say we're not in a position to bargain.>

But Gonrod had recovered. <I command, here. Am I clear on that?>

"No, sir. This is Earth. This is a human planet. We are not the Hork-Bajir. We know how you 'rescued them.' As long as you're on Earth, you'll get along with us. Am I clear on that?"

Fool. An embarrassment. Gonrod was behaving very badly. What was the point in this? I looked at Estrid. She refused to acknowledge me. But I could see the evidence on her face that she, too, was humiliated by this ludicrous display.

For his part, Aloth was a seemingly straightforward warrior. He was awaiting orders, his expression professionally blank. Whatever he thought of his commander, he concealed it.

Arbat was a different matter. Arbat's contempt for Gonrod was scarcely camouflaged.

"Now," Prince Jake said, "who are you? Why are you here?"

Gonrod nodded to Arbat and Aloth. They dropped their weapons.

Cassie and Marco withdrew. Not far, but a little, at least. Of course I knew that Rachel and Tobias were still to be accounted for.

I lowered my tail blade and Estrid lowered her shredder.

Arbat stepped forward and spoke. He was an older Andalite. Much of his blue fur was tanned. <After the unexpected victory on Leera, major elements of the fleet were ordered to Earth. But it was diverted to the *Rakkam Garoo* conflict in the Nine-Sifter system.>

<What, are you people on call for every war in the galaxy?> Marco muttered.

"So Earth waits. Again," Prince Jake said. "You're not the fleet, so who are you?"

<Unit O. A sabotage and assassination team,> Arbat explained. <Commander Gonrod is one of the ablest pilots in the fleet. Aloth is a warrior.>

<An assassination team? Who is the assassin?>

<I am,> Aloth said.

I tried not to stare at him. I had never met an assassin. I had not known any existed in the Andalite military. The notion of such a thing did not make me comfortable.

<And I am an Apex Level Intelligence Advisor. Veteran of over twenty conflicts,> Arbat finished. <Gonrod is in overall command of the mission. I will direct the specific actions of terminating the target.>

I automatically straightened my shoulders. Apex Level Intelligence is the highest level of advisory to the War Council. Not soldiers, precisely. They are military adjuncts. Strategists. They plotted. They planned.

And they knew everything.

Did Arbat know the truth about Elfangor? About me? Likely. Our eyes met, but I could read nothing in their ironic, self-possessed gaze.

Gonrod was a fool. Arbat was not.

"What about Estrid?" Prince Jake asked.

Gonrod looked slightly embarrassed. <Female *arisths* are a new addition to the military. She was assigned to this mission by accident.>

Estrid's four eyes stared at blank space. Blinked rapidly. A sign of embarrassment. I felt sorry for her.

"In other words, she's a rookie?" Jake said.

Estrid lifted her head. <I have trained hard,> she replied in a steely tone. <Make no mistake. I intend to carry my weight.>

Fwapp!

I reeled as the force of her small, female tail blade caught the side of my neck, knocking me off balance.

While I struggled to keep my footing, a second blow caught me behind the back legs, causing my knees to buckle. My rear end fell to the ground and pinned my tail beneath me.

Fwapp!

A third blow sent my front end sprawling. I tried to break my fall with my hands. But Andalite arms are not as strong as human arms. I fell, my chin scraping the grass.

CHAPTER 10

Estrid placed her front left hoof on my throat. <Any questions?>

<Very impressive,> I conceded.

It was a classic and beautifully executed *hald-wurra*. Old Andalite for "victory in three swipes."

She removed her hoof and reached down to assist me. I took her hand. Sprang to my feet. Pulled her arm behind her back and lifted my tail blade just in time to block her defensive swipe.

There was a loud clatter as our blades clashed. I released her arm and disengaged my tail. Sprang backward.

<I am betting on Aximili.> Aloth eagerly stepped forward to get a better view.

<You are a fool,> Arbat told him. <She will have him in two moves. But I accept the wager.>

WHOOSH!

I pulled my head back. Her tail blade, turned to present the dull edge, missed my throat by centimeters.

"Ax?" Prince Jake's voice was full of genuine alarm.

<Please do not interfere,> I said abruptly. I swung my tail hard. Not as hard as I could.

She drew back her head, just as I expected, allowing my tail to double back with even more momentum and speed. As it neared her head, I turned it so that the flat side caught her.

The blow caught her off guard. She tumbled to the ground. Rolled and sprang up nimbly again.

She was not going to be easily defeated. <You have a good swing,> she said. <But mine is better.>

Fwapp! Fwapp!

She was right. I had never seen a tail move so fast. In the blink of an eye, she caught me with the exact same move. This time I fell and rolled. Sprang up. Not as nimbly.

<Ooh, that had to hurt,> Marco commented.

<You did that very gracefully,> Estrid observed.

I was glad my fatigue had not shown. <Thank you. You will not see me do it again.>

She laughed. <You hope.>

CLANG!

She blocked my tail blade with hers. The impact of the blades rang out through the trees.

I began to fear I might actually lose. It would be unbearably humiliating in front of Andalite officers.

<Go, Ax-man!> Tobias yelled from wherever he was hiding.

We sprang apart, both of us breathing hard. She lowered her head and raced straight at me. I leaped out of the way and she sideswiped me. I was knocked at an angle.

It took me a moment to recover. And to remember something I had been taught on the first day of my training.

Estrid bucked forward, preparing to pivot on her front legs and deliver another tail blow. I pivoted, too, turning out of the way.

She missed me. Overshot. The weight and momentum of her tail sent her tumbling forward. She rolled over her head and neck and landed on her back with a cry of pain.

Arbat ran forward. <Estrid!>

She lay still for a moment. Then she began to laugh. <You beat me with the simplest move in the lexicon.>

<Sometimes the simplest solutions are the most effective,> I replied.

If she had been a male, I would have begun to boast. But it seemed less than gracious to boast about beating a female. Even one who was very, very good.

Aloth chuckled happily. He had won his bet.

Prince Jake watched me with a frown. He shook his head slightly and rolled his eyes upward. It is a human expression with several interpretations. In this case I believe my prince thought I was behaving foolishly.

I would have helped Estrid, but Arbat was already pulling her to her feet.

<I apologize,> she said to him. <You have lost your bet.>

<You fought well,> he said proudly. He looked at me with new respect in his eyes. <But you fought better. You have not forgotten your academy training. And you show the sign of a great deal of experience.>

<There have been battles,> I said.

Arbat gave me a speculative look. <I believe we have common goals, Aximili. I believe you and I have much in common. Visser Three killed your brother. What Visser Three did to my brother was worse than death.>

"What did he do?" Prince Jake asked.

Arbat's face betrayed no emotion. <My brother is Alloran. Host body to Visser Three.>

I was not equally controlled. I jerked involuntarily.

Prince Jake's eye narrowed. "So you're here to . . ."

<To assassinate him,> Arbat answered. <Yes. Our mission is to kill Visser Three.>

CHAPTER 11

"Revenge is pointless and immoral," Cassie insisted.

"Revenge is just another word for justice," Rachel said, her face hardening.

"He's talking about killing his own brother," Cassie argued.

"He had a chance. Back at the newspaper," Marco said.

"He wasn't prepared," Rachel argued.

"Visser Three doesn't give a lot of second chances," Marco said. "Maybe these guys are just blowing smoke. Maybe Arbat isn't as bad as he thinks he is. Although Aloth looks like trouble."

I watched a group of grackles pecking at

some spilled seed. One appeared not to be hungry. Instead of strutting and circling, he stood to the side, staring about him with an unwinking eye.

<Does that grackle appear ill?> I asked Cassie.

Cassie looked at the bird and frowned. "I can't tell."

The bird flapped its wings and flew up into the rafters. Walked vigorously along the hayloft, pecking at stray straws.

"Looks healthy to me," Rachel said.

"Forget the birds," Marco snapped. "We have some stuff to deal with here."

He was right, of course. At least about the importance of the issue. I hoped he was not right about Arbat.

Arbat had revealed that Visser Three occupied his brother's body. I understood why Arbat had hesitated when he had the chance to kill the visser. I understood. I sympathized.

And yet, I worried.

Any Andalite — and many humans — would rather die than continue to serve as host. But to perform the killing or not is an agonizing decision. As it should and must be.

Marco's mother is a Controller.

Prince Jake's brother, Tom, is also a human-Controller.

I did not tell Arbat that I, too, had been unable to kill Alloran. Not even when the former war prince had begged me for death as the slug that was Visser Three temporarily abandoned Alloran's poisoned body.

I could not. To my unending shame, I could not bring myself to kill him. And just as Alloran had feared, the Yeerks had revived him. Visser Three had reinfested him.

So we had listened as Arbat explained Unit O's mission.

The War Council had ordered Visser Three killed. Visser Three was a continuing embarrassment to our people. We had allowed him to keep an Andalite host and had been unable to stop him.

Visser Three was an enemy. We were at war. It made sense.

But why had Arbat been chosen for the mission? Surely it must have occurred to someone that organizing and ordering the death of his brother was a particularly difficult thing for him to do.

"War is one thing," Cassie said now. "Murder is another. What do we gain by helping Arbat and Aloth assassinate the visser?"

I spoke. <By Andalite custom, the murder of a family member must be avenged. Perhaps together, Arbat and Aloth and I can succeed where each of us alone has failed.>

"Sounds like a plan to me," Rachel said.

"It's a terrible plan. Don't help him, Ax," Cassie begged. "Alloran is still alive. Where there's life there's hope."

"Great cliché," Marco sneered.

<An Andalite warrior would rather die than serve as a Yeerk host,> I said.

<I guess it's a live-free-or-die thing,> Tobias said quietly. He sat on a rail overhead.

"Well, it's just cowardly," Cassie insisted, putting her hands on her hips. "The easy way out. If you're dead, you don't have to fight for your freedom, do you?"

There was a long silence. No one said anything. I looked to Prince Jake, but he was sitting with his head in his hands.

"Jake?" Cassie said.

No answer.

Marco stood impatiently. "Are we all in denial or what? Why are we even arguing about this like it matters? I mean come on. We know what this is about. We're sitting here fighting out the same disagreements, asking ourselves what we should do next. There is no next. It's over. It's so over, isn't it? I mean, we fight because we think the Andalites are coming someday, someday. We've been carrying out a delaying action. Slowing the Yeerks down so it wouldn't be too late by the time the big deal Andalites came along."

Rachel let out an exhausted sigh. "As much as I hate to admit it, Marco's right. The fleet is not coming to the rescue. The Andalites aren't here to help save Earth. They're here so Arbat and the Andalite command can settle their score with the visser. This isn't the Marines storming in to save us."

"Exactly!" Cassie said. "It's personal. It's political. But there's no strategic value to the mission. No real military advantage. So that just makes it murder."

"Hey, Cassie, you know what?" Marco snapped. "Who cares? I mean, who cares about all your moralizing? Are you even paying attention? What do you think, that the six of us are going to win this war? By ourselves? Four kids, a bird, and an alien? Six kids who can turn into animals, big deal! We've hurt the Yeerks, we've frustrated them, we've slowed them down, but we're pebbles in their shoes. This has always been about us being the resistance until the Andalites could do a D-Day and save our sorry butts."

I had never heard Marco speak so harshly to Cassie. But more shocking still was that Jake did not step in to silence him.

I had been so distracted by Estrid, by seeing my own people again that I had overlooked how devastating this news would be to my friends. They had hoped for salvation. Instead they were presented with another complex problem, more dangers, more futility.

I scanned each of their faces with my stalk eyes. These were not the humans I had known for so long.

Prince Jake stood. "If the Andalites were serious about helping us, they'd have sent an invading force. And Cassie's right, they trade Visser Three for some other visser, how does that help us? And Marco's right, too. We're tired. We're so tired there are times I don't think I can get up the energy to breathe. And now, instead of help, big-time help, we have what are obviously the dregs of the Andalite forces. Gonrod's a fool. Aloth is just a foot soldier. Estrid's a rookie. And Arbat's a guy off on his own."

"So what's our plan?" Rachel demanded.

Prince Jake said nothing.

It was sad. That is what I realized. Very sad. We had turned to Prince Jake so many times and always he had been there with an answer, a plan, or at least a hope.

Marco slapped Rachel lightly on each cheek. "Wise up. Any plans we had — or have — are basically worth squat at this point. The war is over. Earth lost."

The explosion was instantaneous.

Rachel lunged for Marco. "Don't you EVER touch me again!" she screamed.

Marco fell to the ground and shielded his face with his arms. "Get off me. Get off me, you wacko!"

"Stop it! Stop it!" Cassie cried.

Tobias fluttered to the ground. Laughed bitterly. <That's it. I can't take this anymore. I'm losing my mind. I'm out. Out of *here*, out of *this*, I'm done, man.> Tobias flapped his wings and flew from the barn.

CHAPTER 12

"All right, stop it, Rachel!" Prince Jake pulled her off Marco. Shook her hard.

Rachel reeled back and raked her hair from her eyes.

Marco stumbled to his feet. "Face facts," he panted. "The Andalites don't care. This isn't about Earth. It's about boosting Andalite morale by wasting the guy who made an Andalite a host."

There was a long silence. Everyone looked at me. Staring as if they expected — hoped — that I would deny the truth of what Marco was saying.

"Ax?" Prince Jake prompted.

I shook my head. What was there to say?

Prince Jake frowned. "Then what do we want to do?"

"I know what I'm going to do." Rachel angrily kicked a metal bucket. It clattered along the dirt floor of the barn.

Two injured geese sent up an alarmed gabble. A small brown rabbit who had been sitting beside a bale of hay dove into a stall and disappeared from sight.

Five or six grackles who had been pecking in the dirt squawked and flew up into the rafters.

"Rachel," Cassie said quietly, putting her hand on Rachel's arm. "Please. We need you."

Rachel jerked her arm from Cassie's grasp. "From now on I'm doing it my way. No more Geneva Convention warfare. If I'm going down, I'm taking out all the Yeerks I can before I go."

She stalked toward the door.

"Rachel!" Prince Jake shouted.

Rachel whirled around. Her face red with anger. "I'm through taking orders from you," she said through clenched teeth. "I'm through with Marco and his stupid jokes. I'm through with Cassie's hypocrisy."

Rachel lifted her fist and punched a lantern hanging from a hook. The glass splintered and it fell to the ground.

"I'm through with all of you," she hissed. And stormed from the barn.

Cassie took a broom from the corner and began to sweep up the glass. “Count me out, too,” she said softly. “If this war is unwinnable, how do we justify killing Hork-Bajir? Basically, they’re prisoners of war. Innocent victims.”

“Cassie,” Prince Jake pleaded.

A tear rolled down her cheek. “I can’t do it anymore.” She dropped the broom and ran from the barn.

Marco thrust his hands into his pockets. “Guess I’m out, too. I’m going to enjoy what time I’ve got left. Acquire a surfer dude chick magnet. Hang out.”

“Marco,” Prince Jake whispered. “Please.”

Marco put his hand on Prince Jake’s shoulder. Let it slip off as he backed away. “Jake. Ax-man. Live long and prosper.”

Prince Jake and I were alone.

We looked at one another. <I am still yours to command.> I offered him my hand to shake as humans do.

Prince Jake gripped it. His eyes were sad. “I can’t hold you to your oath. The others are right. It’s over. Go on. Do what you have to do. And if you can, go home.”

Prince Jake squeezed my hand tightly, forgetting that Andalite hands are not as strong as human hands. I knew it was an expression of affection. I tried to return the pressure.

Prince Jake straightened his shoulders and lifted his chin. “Good-bye,” he said. “And thank you. For everything.”

He walked slowly from the barn. His silhouette disappeared into the bright glare of the morning sun.

I stood alone.

Remembering.

It was peaceful for the first time in a long time. No arguments or debates. Quite pleasant, really.

<Estrid,> I said finally. <If you are going to acquire Earth morphs, you must learn how to use them. Rabbits do not commonly chase large four-footed creatures like myself across a field and then into a barn full of shouting humans.>

Under the bottom slat of a stall gate, the small brown rabbit appeared. Estrid quickly de-morphed and blinked with embarrassment at her mistake. <I have much to learn.>

<I will teach you,> I said simply.

Her four eyes looked at me and shone. <You will be happier with your own kind.>

CHAPTER 13

The Andalite ship was cloaked in a large empty field outside the fence of a family entertainment center called The Gardens. I knew The Gardens well. Within it was a zoo where Prince Jake, the others, and I had acquired a number of useful morphs.

We flew there from the barn. Before we left, Estrid acquired an Earth bird morph. A crow. We flew, but far enough apart to allay suspicion.

As we descended, a square "hole" appeared in the sky. The upper hatch of the ship. We flew inside and it slid shut behind us.

<This is the upper deck,> Estrid explained. <Let us demorph and I will take you down to the command deck.>

We demorphed and she led me through the hallways and corridors that connected what seemed to be several wings. It was large for a warship. Small for a transport.

<This ship is designated the *Crusader*. It's an MSTL-37,> she explained. <A Mobile Science and Technology Lab ship. Pretty much obsolete by now.>

<An odd choice of ship to send on such a mission.>

She shrugged. <It was what they could spare. The fighters and transports were needed in Nine-Sifter.>

We stood in front of a drop shaft and waited for the doors to open. <Estrid, I would like to ask a favor of you.>

Her four eyes looked curiously at my face.

<I still respect my former prince. We fought many battles together. I would appreciate if you would refrain from reporting that he was unable to maintain control of his warriors. I would not want the others to lose their respect for him. He has fought a good fight.>

<You kept my secret. I will keep yours.>

The drop-shaft door opened and I stepped in beside her.

I was uneasy. My request had been a test. But I was not sure whether she had passed or failed.

I felt grateful for her willingness to protect my prince.

But what kind of an *aristh* would agree to withhold sensitive intelligence information from her superiors?

Had she been instructed to gain my trust in order to spy on me?

Or was she simply undertrained? Unsuited to the military because of her gender?

I resolved to keep my guard up and my eyes open. I watched her fingers dance across a control panel as she programmed in an access code for me.

Her hands were small. And graceful. When she was done, she turned her four eyes on me. My heart rates accelerated.

I had noticed her four eyes staring at me quite a bit.

That, too, was odd.

The first lesson every *aristh* learned at the academy was: "Two eyes out front. Two eyes scanning." Always. A soldier never, ever, focused all his attention on the same spot.

The shaft dropped us two decks and held us there. We stepped out onto the command deck. Gonrod, Aloth, and Arbat were waiting.

<Aximili!> Arbat stepped forward to greet me. His voice was welcoming.

I saluted and made the traditional Andalite bow. <Commander Gonrod. My prince has released me and I now pledge myself to you.>

Gonrod appeared mollified by the respect I showed him.

<We are quite informal on this mission,> Arbat said.

Gonrod bristled. <But the chain of command is clear.>

<Of course. Of course,> Arbat said to Gonrod. <I did not mean to imply otherwise.>

Arbat walked over to a workstation where Aloth calibrated a collection of handheld shredders. <With one of these, I hope to destroy Visser Three.>

<How can I help?> I asked him.

Arbat took my arm. Guided me to the terraced perimeter of the deck where we could look out through the windows at the barren scrub grass outside. He thought-spoke to me privately. <I am willing to do anything it takes to destroy Visser Three. Are you?>

<I look forward to the day when Visser Three no longer threatens free people,> I answered guardedly.

<I trust you, Aximili. You have done well to survive here. I hope to benefit from your advice and experience.>

I shifted my weight uneasily. An Apex Level

Intelligence Advisor is the highest rank in the intelligence division. An *aristh* the lowest rank in the regular military. On Earth I had followed, not led. Nor had I succeeded in killing Visser Three. Additionally, I had violated — by word and deed — more Andalite military codes than I could count.

So why was Arbat treating me with such elaborate respect? Respect that I had not earned by Andalite standards.

He wanted something from me.

But what?

CHAPTER 14

Arbat broke off when he heard the heavy clop of Aloth's hooves approach.

<*Aristh* Aximili,> said Aloth. <Commander Gonrod has asked me to show you around the ship.>

<Excellent!> Arbat beamed. <Show our new comrade around.>

I saluted Arbat and quickly followed the assassin down the corridor.

<If I hear one more war story from that old wind machine I may have to self-destruct,> Aloth said when the shaft doors closed behind us.

I was shocked. But I could not help chuckling. <How can you talk that way about an Apex Level Intelligence Advisor?>

Aloth snorted. <And retired for the last six wars! He's a teacher now! A professor of technological history.>

Like many soldiers, Aloth had little respect for anyone who was not a soldier.

<He teaches at the academy?> I asked.

<No! At the University of Advanced Scientific Theory.>

The UAST was full of brilliant thinkers. But they were notorious for their impracticality. Not known for their battlefield skills.

It seemed very strange that the War Council would send an aging professor of technological history to direct an assassination.

But then, the military had obviously undergone many changes since I left the home planet. <Female *aristh*s. Have they worked out well?>

Aloth snorted again. <I keep waiting for Estrid to find some way of making herself useful.>

<Does she have no duties?>

Aloth shrugged. <None that seem necessary. Gonrod and I both tried to make a detour and drop her at a base. But Arbat was adamant that she remain on board.>

<Why?>

He shrugged. <I cannot think of any reason why he would want an inexperienced female *aristh* on a mission like this. Especially one who is not exactly regulation issue. She behaves more

like a princess than an *aristh*. And Arbat treats her that way.>

Aloth's lazy insolence was gone now. He seemed lost in troubled thought.

<Does her presence concern you?> I ventured, prepared for him to snub me. He did not.

Instead, he resumed his lazy warrior's swagger. <I suppose not. She is probably here because inter-gender staffing is some pet project Arbat sold the War Council on. Or maybe she is somebody's niece and he got her fast-tracked through the academy.>

Aloth gave me a significant look and laughed cynically. I had the feeling I had just missed something. But if that were true about Estrid, it would explain many things.

<I guess none of us are exactly what you would call "regulation issue,"> Aloth added with a wry laugh.

<No? What do you mean by that?>

<Nothing I feel like explaining to an *aristh*,> he said with a chuckle. <Not even the brother of Elfangor. Now stop asking me questions and listen for a change. You might learn something.>

This was the dynamic I understood. The good-natured snubbing a lowly *aristh* would expect from an experienced warrior.

<We are on the third tier. There is the engine room. Storage. Quarters. Yours are at the end.>

<What is on the second tier?>

<Nothing. Used to be a lab. Now it is sealed up so we do not have to waste energy on environmental adaptation conversion. Think you can get around without getting lost?>

<I believe I can. Where is my action station in the event the ship comes under attack?>

Aloth shrugged. <This ship does not have enough firepower to stop a broken-down Skrit Na freighter. If a hot Bug fighter comes after us . . . put it this way: If we're attacked your action station is kissing your tail good-bye.>

Aloth laughed cynically. I did not see the humor.

<Come on. That is the tour. Let us go back to the command deck. The old wheeze wants to "debrief you.">

CHAPTER 15

Moments later Gonrod, Aloth, Arbat, and I met on the command deck. Estrid was not present.

<Tell us about Visser Three.> Arbat seemed eager. Gonrod less so. <Where is he when he is not on his Blade ship?>

<I do not know,> I answered. <How did you find him in the newspaper office?>

<We did not,> Arbat said. <We found you. Our ship sensors were programmed to locate your DNA pattern. We were able to download it from your academy records.>

<Could we not do the same with Alloran's?> I asked.

<Alloran's from the old days. Back before we used DNA encryption.>

<I see. Then our most likely means of finding him would be at the next meeting of The Sharing at the Community Center. He often attends. Not always. But often. Failing that, he is often in the Yeerk pool complex.>

I explained what The Sharing was, and how Visser Three was often present in human morph to address those who attended. I told them also about the location of the Yeerk pool.

<How many Yeerks would be present at the meeting?> Arbat asked.

<We are only interested in one Yeerk,> Gonrod snapped. <Our orders are clear and specific. One target. And then we are done. If Aloth can hit the target.>

<Aloth will hit the target,> Arbat said coldly.

<Will I? It is not an easy thing to do,> Aloth said. <Take aim at a target, a living target, aim for the kill, fire, watch to see the damage. Take a life. And this is no ordinary target, Arbat, but your brother. I have a brother, too. I wonder, when the time comes, whether you will find it so easy to give the final order.>

Arbat ignored Aloth. Or tried to.

<It is a question we would all like answered,> Gonrod said.

<It is a question that will be answered when I give that order and rid the galaxy of the Abomination,> Arbat snapped. It was the first time I had seem him lose what my human friends would call "his cool."

He recovered quickly. <I need as much information as I can gather. May I continue with the questioning of this *aristh*?>

<Very well.> Gonrod's permission was grudging. He peered nervously at the various surveillance screens. It was something he did every few seconds. He seemed extraordinarily ill at ease for a commander.

<The Yeerk pool? Would it be possible to gain access?> Arbat pressed.

<We will not go there!> Gonrod insisted shrilly.

Aloth suppressed a snicker.

Gonrod threw Aloth a belligerent look. <The *aristh* has presented us with a perfectly good target. We will attack this meeting of The Sharing. Tomorrow morning. We will hit Visser Three. And we will leave.>

Arbat opened his hands, as if appealing to Gonrod's reason. <Commander, if the targets were enlarged, and we were to kill many, perhaps thousands, of Yeerks, surely that would be preferable.>

<There will be no enlargement of the target!> Gonrod snapped. <We carry out our orders. And then we leave.>

I saw Estrid in the arched doorway that led to the exit corridor. <Commander Gonrod,> she announced. <I am going on a tour of The Gardens and would like Aximili to accompany me. He can familiarize me with Earth creatures.>

I drew in my breath. I had never heard an *aristh* "announce" his plans and desires to a superior officer. Typically, he waited for orders.

Gonrod's eye stalks quivered angrily.

Estrid appeared to have no idea she had committed a breach of military conduct.

I watched unhappily. I hated to see her rebuked.

Strangely, Gonrod did not do so. <Very well,> he answered curtly.

<Come, Aximili,> she said happily.

I followed her to the exit hatch. The Earth hour was late. The Gardens were closed. There were no humans to watch us disembark and descend to the ground on the cloaked ramp.

Still, I was uneasy.

Estrid was beautiful. She was a well-trained fighter.

But she was no soldier.

Who was she?

CHAPTER 16

In the daytime pigeons and squirrels crowded the walkways of The Gardens.

But at night the sidewalks are clear. There was no sound except our eight hooves clopping slowly along. Normally I might have worried about security personnel spotting us. But of course Estrid knew nothing about this. And I was confident that we would not be bothered.

<Arbat says Earth has more variety of species than any other known planet. When we scanned DNA patterns for you the computers were nearly overwhelmed.>

<Tell me about Arbat and Gonrod,> I said.

<Arbat says Gonrod is an excellent pilot. And that Aloth scored the highest target impact rate

in the history of the academy. Arbat says he's a top sniper.>

<Arbat says.> Again.

Suddenly, I understood. How could I have been so obtuse?

Estrid was Arbat's niece! Of course. That was what Aloth had been hinting.

Arbat might now be a professor of technological history, but he was still Apex Level Intelligence. He whipped a big tail at the War Council.

No wonder Estrid was allowed so much license.

Estrid's four eyes looked to me. <I wonder . . .>

<Yes?>

<The pellets called jelly beans. I would love to taste them again before leaving Earth.>

<I believe we could find some pellets close by.>

Side by side, we trotted through the cool, dark night toward the main building. The Visitors' Center. Outside the building was something Jake and Marco called a "vending machine." A large glass box containing delicious foods.

No cinnamon buns or jelly beans. But many other things that would delight Estrid.

I turned and delivered a kick to the machine. Brightly colored packets fell from hooks inside the machine down into a bin into which I was able to reach.

It was probably not a good thing to do. Humans are very touchy about ownership.

<What are they?> Estrid asked.

<You will enjoy them,> I promised, beginning to morph to human.

Estrid's eye stalks receded into her skull. Her legs and arms retracted. She lay on the ground, a round ball of blue-and-tan fur.

The fur disappeared and became smooth and pink. Then, with one burst, the round ball became a human. Fully clothed. In what humans would consider normal clothing.

I was amazed. I had never seen such an efficient morph. And the ability to morph something other than skintight bicycle shorts and T-shirts took almost supernatural powers of concentration.

"You are an *estreen* . . . nuh," I said.

"My mmmmmother . . . ruh. She was a morph . . . ph dan . . . dancer . . . ruh! Dancer-uh. I learned much from herrrrr!"

I opened one of the packets and poured the contents into her palm.

She popped them into her mouth and her face began to glow. "Bright pellets . . . ssss. Wonderful . . . ful-luh. Jelly beanssssuuhh. More. More."

I poured the rest of them into her hand. "Not jelly beansuh. M&M's. The flavor is called chocolate. Chock-lut."

She laughed. "Mouth-speaking is very amusing. Uh Mew Zing."

"Yes, mouths are very interesting. M&M's. Chock-lut. Watch this . . ."

I stuck out my tongue and let it rest lightly on my upper lip. Then I blew out my breath. "Thhhhbbbbbbbbbb!!!"

Estrid shrieked with laughter.

I did it again. "Thhhhbbbbbbb!!!"

"What does it mean?" she gasped.

"It is called a raspberry," I said. "I do not know why."

"It would be very hard . . . hard-duh to have a mouth all the time. Tie-yem. Time-uh. It would be very difficult to concentrate on a plintconarhythmic equation for more than two minutes. One would be too busy tasting chocolate and making rasp . . . berries . . . suh!"

"Thhhhhbbbbbbb!" The vibrations made my lips tingle.

She leaned close, watching my mouth intently. So close I could feel the tendrils of her human curls tickling my face.

"They have another use for mouths," I said.

"In addition to eating and making mouth-sounds?"

"Yes. Would you like to experience it?"

"Is it pleasurable?" she asked.

I shrugged my large human shoulders. "I do

not know. I have never performed the action before. It requires two individuals, each possessing a minimum of one mouth."

"Let us experiment. Ment. Expeeeeriment."

I took Estrid's face in my hands and I pressed my lips against hers.

I have no words to describe the sensation.

It did not tickle the mouth or cause my lips to tingle.

It caused a chaotic flutter in my stomach. Small bumps broke out up and down my arms. I only had one heart now, but it thundered.

I pulled away.

"That was pleasant," Estrid said. "But not as pleasant as chocolate."

"No. But pleasurable," I said.

"Yes."

"Yes."

CHAPTER 17

Later, Estrid and I flew through the night. Side by side. This, too, was pleasurable.

I almost wished we could spend the rest of our lives like this. Together. Free. No more war. No more duty. No more fear.

It was possible. If we remained in morph beyond two hours, we would become *nothlits*, like Tobias. We could go where we would never be found.

Not by the Yeerks. Not by the Andalites. And not by the Animorphs.

For one brief moment, I considered it.

<Where are we going?> she asked.

I remembered the way she had looked at me

as we kissed. With admiration? Trust? Some other emotion?

We could simply fly away. We could become something or someone else. Life would no doubt be simpler. Life would be a matter of life or death, survival or failure, simple, black or white choices.

But in reality life seldom comes in simple shades of black and white. The choices in the real world, the choices we most often face, are all in shades of gray. And I lived in the real world.

<I would like to see my old friends once more,> I said.

<Why?>

<We were together through more battles than I can count,> I said. <They are no longer my comrades in arms. But I am not indifferent to them.>

<Loyalty is admirable,> she said.

<Yes. It is,> I said dejectedly.

We flew over town toward the barn. Over the mall. Past the school. Over a cluster of stores and restaurants. I took my time.

Then, <Oh, no! Estrid, circle down with me, but remain at a safe distance.>

A terrible spectacle was unfolding below. In the parking lot of a McDonald's a grizzly bear was terrorizing a group of humans.

<It is Rachel,> I told Estrid sadly. <The angry one.>

The teenagers ran screaming into the restaurant.

Rachel lumbered through the parking lot.

BLAM! BLAM! CRASH!

One by one, she bashed in windshields and windows, slammed foot-deep dents into the sheet metal. Horns and alarms wailed.

Whooo-OOP! Whooo-OOP!

SKKareeeeee!

Rachel raged through the restaurant door.

The people inside screamed in terror. Broke windows. Poured back into the parking lot.

<What is she doing?> Estrid asked. <Are those human-Controllers?>

<The restaurant is managed by a human-Controller,> I answered. <I do not know about the other humans. I fear her destruction is indiscriminate. Prince Jake would never have allowed it.>

I saw someone else come out of the restaurant.

Cassie.

She ran into the shadows and disappeared.

Moments later, an owl emerged from the darkness and swooped into the sky.

<Hurry.> We followed Cassie from a distance. She flew back to the barn.

Estrid and I flew quietly through a hole in the

roof and perched on a beam where we could watch without being seen.

Marco lay on top of several bales of hay. He was drinking a soda and reading a magazine.

"Marco!" Cassie cried, in human form now. "You've got to help me. Rachel's going totally postal at McDonald's."

"Not my problem. Me, I like Burger King."

Cassie snatched the magazine from Marco's hands. "She's going to kill somebody."

"What's it to you? I thought you were out of this."

"We can't just stand by while innocent people get hurt."

Marco shrugged. "Speak for yourself."

"Where is Jake?" Cassie demanded. "He'll help me."

Marco took the magazine from Cassie's hand and reclined again. "Don't count on it."

"Why? Where is he?"

"I'm in here," a voice answered.

Cassie peered over the door of one of the stalls. "Jake! What are you doing there?"

Prince Jake's head emerged. "Hiding. Tom's been picking on me all afternoon. I can't take it anymore."

"Then fight back!" Cassie cried.

Marco snickered. "Whoaaa! What happened to our resident nonviolence advocate?"

"Shut *up*, Marco!" she yelled. "Jake! Are you going to help me or not?"

Two grackles in the rafters attacked a third, driving it away. Jake jumped and dove back down into the stall.

"Not." Marco smirked and continued reading.

"What about Rachel?" Cassie cried, her voice breaking.

Marco yawned. "Listen, if she shows at the beach tomorrow, I'll talk to her. Now, why spoil her fun?"

Cassie stood for a moment, shaking with fury. "YOU JERKS!" she screamed. "GET OUT!"

<I have seen enough,> I told Estrid. We quietly made our way out of the hole in the barn roof, and took wing.

<I pity you, Aximili,> Estrid said. <How did you endure it? How could you bear to live among such inferior creatures?>

<They have fought well in the past. But they are demoralized by the prospect of certain defeat.>

Her voice was skeptical. <Perhaps. But no Andalite would behave so. Even in defeat, we are proud.>

She sounded arrogant and vain.

Like me.

CHAPTER 18

<That is the third time tonight I have seen that fierce-looking bird with the sharp beak!> Estrid said.

We were approaching the ship. I looked to where a red-tailed hawk soared high overhead. Above a large grackle.

<Earth has many species of birds,> I reminded her. <And each species can have hundreds of thousands or even millions of members.>

<It looks familiar.>

<Birds all look similar,> I said.

We flew through the hatch. Demorphed and returned to the command deck.

<Where have you been?> Gonrod demanded.

<We went to look over the target site after

touring The Gardens,> Estrid told him. No mention of the barn.

Arbat clopped into the room. <What did you learn?>

Estrid and I drew a simple map of the Community Center. Then Gonrod ordered us to get a good night's rest. We would attack the next morning.

<I would be honored to keep the first watch,> I said.

Gonrod nodded. <Very well. But touch nothing.>

The crew left the deck and disappeared.

The deep humming of the engine and atmospheric adjusters thickened the silence. I was free to think now.

I thought about Estrid. Her grace. Her intelligence. How much I enjoyed watching her in bird morph. How much I enjoyed kissing her in human morph.

I smiled, remembering her delight over the M&M's.

Then my breath caught in my chest.

I had missed something. Something important.

Probably because of my feelings for her.

"It would be very difficult to concentrate on a plintconarhythmic equation for more than two minutes."

Plintconarhythmic physics!

Cutting-edge biochemical engineering. Even Andalite intellectuals do not attempt to learn its elegant but complex formulae and postulates.

They say that no one really understands it. It requires thinking coherently in n-dimensions. It is the plaything of geniuses.

Why would Estrid be concentrating on a plint-conarythmic equation?

<It means nothing,> I told myself. <It is a saying. A pleasantry.> Like when Marco says that something "isn't exactly rocket science." Or when Rachel sneers that someone is a "regular Einstein." Just a phrase to illustrate Estrid's point that taste can be distracting.

Just a saying.

Gonrod told me to touch nothing. Nonetheless, I approached the access unit on the main console.

Estrid's four eyes had been on the control panel when she programmed in my access code. I had watched her fingers.

I would use that code now.

I pulled up the stats on the ship. Estrid was right. An old MSTL-37. Obsolete for scientific research and pressed into service as a medical transport for the wounded and dead in the last two wars.

I tried to call up the personnel records.

A green light began to blink. <ENCRYPTED

DATA! AVAILABLE TO APEX LEVEL CLEARANCE ONLY! ENTER CODE.>

Fwapp!

A tail blade was pressed hard against my throat.

<Spying is a capital offense.> Aloth.

<I am not spying.>

<Then what are you doing?>

<I have forgotten much,> I lied. <I was trying to familiarize myself with the workings of the ship.>

He released me and I let out a long breath of relief.

His stalk eyes perused the screen. He saw the message. His eye stalks slowly turned back toward me. <Trying to familiarize yourself with the ship? Or with your comrades?>

<Both. I would not regard that as spying.>

Aloth slouched against the console. <So. It has begun to occur to you that you have fallen in with a bad crowd? Eh, brother of Elfangor?>

<I am simply curious.>

Aloth looked intensely at me. <I trained for a while under your brother. Different from most princes. Most of them . . . it is almost as if life has never handed them anything but easy grazing. But Elfangor . . . he had lived. You could tell. He had seen things.>

<Yes. He had.> I did not know what else to

say. I did not trust Aloth's intensity. The assassin was a dangerous person.

Aloth laughed his cynical laugh. <You want to know the secrets? You want to know who we are? I will tell you, little Aximili. You know what I was doing before I "volunteered" for this mission?>

<No.>

<Sitting in military prison. Life sentence.>

I took a step back.

<Do not fear me, little *aristh*. I am no danger to *you*. My crime was that I had no use for hypocrisy.>

<Hypocrisy is not illegal.>

<Not all hypocrisy,> he agreed. <If it were, what would we do for leaders? They would all be in jail. Now me, I was caught selling organs. Off the battlefield. They are of no use to the dead, right? Why should someone not make use of them? And why should I not receive something for my trouble?>

The Andalite Battle Code prohibits the selling of organs off the battlefield. It might encourage the less scrupulous to hasten a comrade's end. Or cause it.

A crack shot and a sniper could ensure a steady supply of organs. No wonder he had been sentenced to life.

I was careful not to let my disgust show.

<Yes, you see, *Aristh* Aximili, I am not a hero of the people. But at least I am not a coward.>

<Are you saying I am?>

He laughed. Surprised. <You? No, I meant Gonrod. He was in the same prison as me, though he faced a lesser sentence. His crime was cowardice under fire.>

A coward and a murderer. Both Andalite officers. Were these "my own kind"?

<We were offered the promise of pardon if we successfully completed this mission,> Aloth continued.

<And what about Arbat?>

The assassin shook his head. <As far as I know, he is here to assassinate Visser Three. Gonrod is a coward, but an excellent pilot. His job was to get us here in a substandard ship. Mine is to kill Visser Three if Arbat can get me close enough to do so. With your help Arbat may succeed. Meaning that I succeed.>

<I see. That makes sense.>

<Does it? I am not sure anything makes sense on this mission.>

I did not have anything to say to that. But I had a question. <Aloth, who is really in command of this unit? Arbat? Gonrod? Or is it you?>

Aloth laughed again. <Sometimes, little *aristh*, I think it is the female.>

CHAPTER 19

<Prepare for landing,> Gonrod instructed.

Our ship hovered over the park. Cloaked, of course. For the last hour we had watched people arrive.

Visser Three's limousine had pulled up to the entrance five Earth minutes earlier.

The ship's sensors had probed the building and given us a map of the Center's interior layout, including one extremely large meeting room.

The sensors had even located what we believed to be yet another entrance to the Yeerk pool. A room that seemed to have no floor. No finite measurable depth.

<I remind you our mission is specific and limited,> Gonrod said. <Aloth and Arbat, go in through

the south door. Stop any guards before they raise the alarm. Aximili and I will do the same at the east entrance. Both halls are long. Any disturbance will not be heard in the main meeting room.>

Aloth handed out shredders. When he gave Arbat his, Aloth said, <You know, Professor, if you get there before me, you can do the job.>

Arbat answered coldly, <If I do, I will.>

<Shall we make a wager on it?>

<No. We will do better than a wager. *I* will kill Visser Three. That is an order, Aloth. You will stand by unless I fail. Is that clear?>

<Arbat, Aloth is a trained sniper. You —> Gonrod began.

Arbat drew his shredder, twisted the power setting, and said, <*Aristh?* Grab that empty data disc. Throw it. Any direction, any speed.>

I did not know whom to obey, what to do. But Gonrod did not countermand the order.

I grabbed the disc. It was the size of a human coin. I threw it with a quick flick of my wrist. It flew over Arbat's shoulder.

Arbat followed it with his stalk eyes, aimed, fired over his shoulder. The disc flamed.

It was not an impossible shot. I might have made it. With practice. But it was an impressive shot nevertheless.

<One does not rise to Apex Level without some basic skills,> Arbat said.

Aloth nodded. <You take the first shot, Professor.>

Aloth handed me a shredder and began carefully checking his own with the slow, practiced ease of a person who had done this many times before.

<What about me?> Estrid said.

<I have decided you will stay on the ship,> Arbat said. <That is to say, Commander Gonrod decided,> he amended.

<I refuse!> she protested hotly.

Gonrod whirled on her. <You refuse an order from your commanding officer?> he thundered.

<But I . . .>

<SILENCE! YOU WILL DO AS YOU ARE ORDERED!>

There was a stunned pause.

It was Arbat who had exploded.

Estrid recoiled slightly. Trembled. But obeyed.

<There is a first,> Aloth said. <The girl actually listening to someone.>

I watched Estrid carefully. She was listening to some private thought-speak from Arbat. She was angry. And something else . . . scared?

Gonrod may have been a failure as a commander, but he was a genuinely great pilot. He laid the ship down to a perfect hover not six inches from the roof of the main building. Had the ship been visible it would have made quite a bizarre sight, a large metal ovoid shape resting like some nesting bird atop the Community Center.

We descended the steep ramp to the gravel roof. The jump to the ground would be easy enough.

It was risky to attack in our own Andalite forms. But it was the only way we could get to the building with our shredders. And there was a military purity about attacking as the Andalite warriors we were.

<Good fortune, everyone,> Gonrod said.

<We will need it,> Aloth said mordantly.

<Let us rock and roll,> I said, and laughed at the meaninglessness of the statement.

Aloth and Arbat galloped swiftly to the south face and leaped over the parapet of the roof. Gonrod and I ran at right angles to them. I leaped, landed easily on the grass below.

Two human-Controllers were on guard.

"Anda —"

Tseeewww! Tseeewww!

They slumped.

Gonrod jerked his head, indicating that I should follow him. I could hear Visser Three. He was in human morph. His powerful voice boomed through the facility.

<That is him,> I said.

We made our way up thickly carpeted steps to the second floor.

Tseeew! Tseeew!

Two more human-Controllers dropped before they could so much as yell.

I began to wonder if we might, just might, manage to do this thing.

The central meeting room was two stories high with a second-floor balcony surrounding it on four sides.

A human-Controller heard us. Turned.

Fwapp!

I hit him, knocked him to his knees, and hit him again to make sure he stayed down for a while.

We looked down from the balcony. Visser Three was on a stage, at the podium. No doubt the podium was shielded, armored. But the upper third of the visser's human morph was in plain view.

I could kill him. I could. Should.

But I felt relieved knowing that Arbat had taken the honor of the first shot. Relieved that I did not have to take aim, squeeze the shot, watch the visser's head flame.

Across the room, on the balcony nearest Visser Three, just above him to his right, I saw three human-Controllers drop. One. Two. The third spun and raised his weapon. And down he went.

Impossible not to feel pride mixed with the fear. Within seconds this gaggle of Andalite rejects had penetrated the Yeerk security. All without an alarm being raised.

But now Visser Three was demorphing. This was a meeting of the Inner Sharing. Controllers all. There were none of the vague, simple fools who clustered in the swimming pool, the game room, the playground, and thought that this organization would give them a sense of belonging they lacked.

These were not the "wanna-be's," as Marco would call them. These were the hard-core.

Visser Three stood there now, an Andalite-Controller. *The* Andalite-Controller.

And Arbat was within twenty feet. An easy shot. A clear shot. He could kill the Abomination.

And his brother.

I knew suddenly, with the clarity that sometimes comes from moments of great stress, that Arbat would miss.

I lifted my shredder and took careful aim.

Tseeewww!

Shredder fire streaked past Visser Three's head.

Arbat had fired.

He'd blown a hole in the curtains gathered on the far side of the stage.

An easy shot.

A miss.

CHAPTER 20

Aloth fired.

Tseeew!

Too late! The visser was down, whipped around behind the podium.

Still in my view. Still in my sights.

Had to fire. He'd murdered Elfangor.

Had to fire.

Aloth fired again. The podium sizzled and jumped with electrical discharge.

Had to . . .

Reinforcements coming. Two Hork-Bajir burst in through a side door. Why were the human-Controllers not firing?

Of course. They were disarmed. The paranoid leader could not stand up there and address a

meeting hall full of armed men, Controllers or not.

Gonrod fired.

The visser's back was seared by the beam.

<Shoot, Aximili, shoot!> I screamed at myself. <Shoot!>

I fired. Did not even know I had, did not realize I had made the decision.

I felt the warmth of the weapon in my hand.

Saw the beam incinerate the stage floor where Visser Three had been just seconds before.

Miss!

No, not a miss. I had waited too long. I had let the moment pass.

The visser was morphing something small. A part of me, a far-off, rational part of me noted that the visser had begun at last to learn that sometimes bigger was not better.

Hork-Bajir bodyguards closed in around the podium. Screaming human-Controllers poured out of the meeting room, emptying it in seconds.

But the meeting room did not stay empty for long. Five doors around the room opened, and in charged a battalion of Hork-Bajir.

Gonrod let out a gasp. A battalion of Hork-Bajir is terrifying to behold.

The Hork-Bajir spotted me and Gonrod on the balcony almost immediately. With surprising agility, they formed a pyramid. Other Hork-Bajir scrambled up to the balcony using their comrades' various blades and horns as steps.

Tseeewww! Tseeewww! Tseeewww! Tseeewww! Tseeewww!

Gonrod fired wildly. In panic. His shots were doing damage, but not enough.

And me? I stood frozen.

Four Hork-Bajir propelled themselves over the balcony railing.

Tseeewww! Tseeewww! Tseeewww! Tseeewww!

Four Hork-Bajir dropped with neatly placed holes through their chests. The bodies fell heavily. Gonrod must have shot. I turned my eye stalk to look. But he was no longer with me.

Aloth! He had come running around the balcony.

Arbat? Where was he? And where was Gonrod?

<Jump!> Aloth yelled.

I snapped out of my trance. Side by side Aloth and I ran down the balcony and hurdled over the side. I landed badly, sprawled amidst chairs. I scrambled up. Nothing broken.

Tseeew! Tseeew!

Aloth fired into the mass of Hork-Bajir.

Above!

Two Hork-Bajir dropping down onto Aloth.

Tseeew!

I fired and hit one in the arm. The other fell hard. I used my tail and dropped him.

Aloth gave me a curt nod. Then, <Let us get out of here, *Aristh.*>

We ran, out through one of the doors. Out into a corridor. Arbat was there. He was firing methodically from left to right, forcing back the Hork-Bajir.

<Arbat! This way. We will cover you!> Aloth yelled.

Aloth and I began to fire into the mass of the enemy. Arbat fell back to join us. The Hork-Bajir were taking cover in doorways.

<Visser Three! He escaped!> Arbat cried.

<Forget Visser Three. The mission is aborted.>

<Where is Gonrod?> I asked.

<I think he is . . .> Aloth looked to the left, momentarily diverting his eye stalks.

Hork-Bajir, behind us!

I spun.

<Arggghhhhh!> Aloth fell heavily, both front knees slashed by a Hork-Bajir. He lifted his weapon but the Hork-Bajir brought his elbow blade down and slashed him from shoulder to hock.

I fired. The Hork-Bajir fell. Then I advanced. Wading in and strafing as I had seen Arbat do.

My tail snapped and whistled as it sliced the hands of a Hork-Bajir who attempted to grab my arm. Other Hork-Bajir drew back in alarm.

Aloth was hurt. Badly. But he could survive.

All he needed was room so he could get up. And out.

The Hork-Bajir began to retreat.

With one eye stalk I watched Aloth climb to his feet.

Tseeewww!

Aloth sank to the floor. He was dead. Shot cleanly through the head.

By Arbat.

An accident?

No. Impossible!

<Retreat!> Arbat ordered, thundering past me.

Aloth was dead. Gonrod probably as well. Arbat was in charge.

Murderer!

My mind reeled. What could I do? The Hork-Bajir were massing for a new charge.

I retreated.

Ran. Ran with my brain replaying it again and again. Arbat had shot Aloth!

Out. Into the air of Earth.

<I have you,> Estrid called tersely from the ship. <Keep going. Just ahead of you!>

The cloaked ship shimmered and appeared, hovering above the playground. Two children and their parents would have a story to tell that no one would believe.

I leaped for the ramp, Arbat right beside me.

The cloak came down.

<Aloth?> Estrid demanded.

<Get us out of here!> Arbat yelled.

The ship powered up and away.

When we reached the command deck, I drew in my breath. Gonrod was already on board. Working frantically at the controls, Estrid beside him.

<I am throwing out plexine vapor over a two-thousand-mile grid,> he said. <That should keep their Blade ship sensors from picking up our atmospheric disruption. Where is Aloth?>

<Aloth is dead,> I told him tightly. <He looked away from the fight — looked for you — and was injured.>

Gonrod yanked a lever. The ship made a sharp vertical ascent. <I thought it best to retreat for strategic reasons.> Gonrod's voice was defensive.

Retreated? Gonrod had run like a coward!

<The record will reflect that you retreated for strategic reasons in order to allow us to escape,> Arbat said as we rocketed upward. <It will also reflect that I terminated Aloth because he was too injured to escape,> he added, holding my gaze.

<He was not!> I protested. <He could have gotten safely back to the ship. With our help.>

<But we could not take that risk, could we?>

Arbat answered smoothly. <We could not take the chance that another Andalite body would become a Yeerk host.>

I shook. With anger. Fear. And with confusion.

Arbat had had two opportunities to kill Visser Three. He had failed in both instances. And he had killed the officer who had been ordered to kill the visser if he did not.

What was going on here? What possible motive could he have for sabotaging his own unit's mission?

Estrid spoke to me. <Aximili. You are upset. Calm yourself.>

<She is right,> Arbat said. <Let us not mourn a fallen warrior. Let us honor his memory by avenging him.>

He turned both eye stalks in my direction. <Now, tell me about the Yeerk pool.>

CHAPTER 21

<We will not attack the pool,> Gonrod insisted as he expertly landed the ship near the pond where we had held our initial meeting.

<We must,> Arbat told him.

<Those are not my orders from the War Council!> Gonrod's voice was almost tearful. <I am in command. I refuse to attack the pool without orders. It is too risky. Do you understand? If we were captured, the Yeerks would have more Andalite hosts. You said so yourself. That is why you killed Aloth.>

Arbat's answer was laced with menace. <Let me remind you that I am Apex Level Intelligence. If I chose to exercise my prerogatives and relieve

you of command, you would then have no choice but to follow my orders.>

<Relieve me? On what grounds?>

<I believe you know.>

Gonrod's voice quivered with indignation. <But the War Council . . .>

<I will take full responsibility,> Arbat assured him. <The War Council and I have — an understanding.>

It was a masterpiece of understatement. The Apex Level of Andalite Intelligence pretty much ran the War Council.

<The *aristh* will lead us in,> Arbat told Gonrod. <Tonight.>

Gonrod did not argue. Estrid remained impassive. She took neither side, but of course, in practical effect, that made her Arbat's ally.

Gonrod landed the ship back at The Gardens. We all agreed that we needed rest. All we could possibly have agreed on at that particular moment.

I went to my quarters. Moments later I was off the ship and in the air.

I needed computer skills well beyond my own. It is one thing to penetrate human computer security — if you can even call it security — it was a different thing altogether to abrogate Apex Level Security measures.

I returned to the ship an hour later. In time for my own watch on deck.

<I am your relief, Gonrod,> I told him.

He seemed far away. Distracted. But he acknowledged me and returned the ritual reply. <A most welcome relief. The ship is yours.>

Gonrod left the deck.

I took a deep breath. Entered myself in the computer as the officer on duty. Then I said, <It is safe.>

The panel of monitors before me shimmered. And out of the image stepped a thing that seemed to be made of steel and ivory. A machine whose form vaguely suggested that of an Earth canine.

The android met my gaze, then shimmered again. Where the android had stood was now a man who called himself Mr. King.

Mr. King. The Chee. Android.

<Your holographic technology is genuinely impressive,> I said. <Thank you for your help.>

"The Chee owe you," he said simply. "Now, let's see about this security system."

He switched off his familiar appearance and reverted to his true form.

<Can you not remain disguised while here? I am concerned that someone may come up here.>

"It's a question of energy demand," he said. "I can stay 'human' and do it slow, or I can divert all energy to the job and get it done faster."

<Faster,> I said.

He pressed a finger into one of the console ports and his joints whirred and clicked. "Here it comes."

I saw the computer screen light up.

<ENCRYPTED DATA! APEX LEVEL CLEARANCE ONLY! ENTER CODE.>

The screen began to blink. Counters appeared. Images scrolled past in a blur.

"Here we go. We're in. Who are we looking for?"

<Start with Aloth-Attamil-Gahar.>

There was a brief pause. Then Aloth's name and record appeared. He was already listed as "Killed in Action."

<Request detail,> I instructed.

A pause.

"He was killed in action in some system called *Rakkam Garoo,*" Mr. King said. "A ship called *Ralek River.* The ship was destroyed."

<I see. Now Gonrod-Isfall-Sonilli.>

Pause.

"Same story. Identical."

<Arbat-Elivat-Estoni?>

Pause.

The android turned his canid face to me. "You have a bunch of unlucky friends. This one was also killed aboard the *Ralek River.*"

<Yes. Quite a coincidence.>

"Is that it?"

<One more name: Estrid-Corill-Darrath?>

Pause.

"No record."

<Try again.>

"Says, 'No record of personnel by that name.'"

<Try accessing the academy files.>

This time the pause was longer.

"Nope," Mr. King said. "Nothing."

I was feeling sick. Scared. Impossible. It was all impossible.

A tired old ship sent on a vital mission staffed by misfits who were already listed as dead.

My hearts began a dull, sickening thud.

The Andalite War Council did not expect this ship to return. The Andalite War Council did not want this ship to return.

This ship was on a suicide mission.

CHAPTER 22

I thanked Mr. King for his assistance and then left the command deck in search of some answers.

I took the drop shaft to the third tier, moving slowly and cautiously. I passed Aloth's empty quarters. Gonrod's door was closed. So was Estrid's, but I knocked softly.

No answer.

I pressed my ear against the door to see if I could hear her stirring. I heard nothing. At least nothing from inside Estrid's room.

A vibration in the wall. Sound conducted by the metal tubing that reinforced the seams of the ship.

I heard the clink of plex against plex. The faint rattle of metal. And then, the sound of hooves.

The sound was traveling up from the second tier. The tier that was supposed to be sealed off. The lab.

I stepped back into the shaft and off at the second tier. The hallway was dark.

I stepped forward and felt the creepy crawly sensation of passing through a force field.

It was easy to figure out what the force field contained. My stomach turned. It smelled like death on this floor. Sour. Putrid. The rot of diseased flesh. The force field kept the stench from permeating the ship.

And no wonder. The wall was lined with casket vaults. Empty now, but still redolent with the hideous odor of death.

I picked up my hooves, careful to make no sound as I made my way toward the source of the faint noises.

The smells of death receded and were replaced by the smell of decontaminant. I stopped outside a door. Yes, she was in there.

I slid the door open manually to minimize noise.

Estrid stood at a lab table, pouring the contents of one plex vial into another. She dropped the first vial into a steaming container of decontaminant and carefully began to place a cap on the second vial.

She saw me. Jerked in surprise. The vial slipped from her hand.

<NO!>

Her terror galvanized me. I dove forward, my back legs skidding on the floor. I fell heavily but reached out my hands and caught the vial.

Estrid groaned and her knees buckled. She sank down. Held a trembling hand out to me. <Give it to me.> Her voice shook. <Please. Carefully.>

<What is it, Estrid?>

Her expression hardened. <That is not your concern.>

I rolled to my feet, still holding the vial.

<Careful!> she cried, scrambling up herself.

I began to open the vial.

<NO!> She lurched forward.

I held it out of reach. <I have grown very tired of being lied to,> I said. <I want the truth.>

<Go ask Arbat.>

<I am asking you.>

<I cannot answer.>

<Ah, but you can,> I said. I held the vial gingerly and twisted open the cap.

<No! You idiot!>

<Question number one: You are not an *aristh*. Are you?>

Her eyes flickered. <No,> she said after a long pause.

<Yes and no,> she amended. <I was made an honorary *aristh* for this mission. But I have never attended the academy.>

I am ashamed to say that my first feeling was one of embarrassment. That a female, one that had never even attended the academy, had very nearly beaten me in one-on-one combat. <If you did not attend the academy, where did you learn your tail fighting?>

<I have a brother,> she explained.

My embarrassment was not alleviated. <I, too, had a brother with whom I tail fought. But it took years of academy training for him to achieve your level of skill.>

<My brother is Ajaht-Litsom-Esth,> she said.

Ajaht-Litsom-Esth! I could not help laughing. Ajaht-Litsom-Esth is the highest scoring exhibition tail fighter on the Andalite planet.

<And are you also Arbat's niece?>

<No. His student. At the University of Advanced Scientific Theory.>

I was astounded. <But you are . . .>

<Young. Yes. I am a prodigy. A genius. I do not mean to sound immodest, but it is true. It has not been easy,> she said softly. <At the university, they treated me as a joke when I arrived.

A young female! So, of course, they forced me into sub-particle fusion.>

The eyes on her face flashed with anger. <I was so intellectually frustrated, I wanted to die. Then I met Arbat.>

Now her eyes shone. <He saw past my youth and my gender. He saw what I could do if I had the freedom and the tools. His influence changed everything. I received my own lab. Permission to follow my own area of interest.>

<Plintconarhythmic physics?>

She nodded.

<Theoretical or applied?>

<Applied.>

<Yes, of course.> Slowly. Carefully. I placed the vial on the counter. <What is it?> I asked, almost certain that I would rather not know.

<A prion virus, of sorts. I would explain, but you . . .>

<No. I would not understand,> I admitted.

<I discovered it. By accident, really. When I confided in Arbat, he sealed off my lab to the rest of the faculty and my research was classified as Apex Level Weapons Intelligence.>

<It is a weapon?>

She nodded. <Three benign particles. In combination, they form a quasi-virus. A programmable virus. Deadly to Yeerks.>

I shivered with revulsion. Germ warfare.

Her eye stalks drooped. <There is one problem,> she continued. <One of the components is subject to . . . to simplify, it has a volatility that could cause it to mutate in a Yeerk with a human host.>

<Meaning?>

<Meaning it could become deadly to humans also.>

CHAPTER 23

Now it was all clear. Crystal clear.

Gonrod and Aloth were dupes. This mission was about Arbat and Estrid. Gonrod was an expendable pilot. Aloth? A thug.

The War Council sent them to Earth with the understanding that their mission was to assassinate Visser Three.

The reality was that Estrid and Arbat were here on a genocidal errand for which no one on the War Council was willing to take official responsibility. Not after the disaster on the Hork-Bajir planet.

In fact, the War Council might know nothing of this mission at all. Was Arbat a renegade?

No wonder Arbat had not wanted Visser Three

assassinated. Had Aloth successfully killed him, Gonrod would have been forced to report "mission accomplished" over the secure communication channels.

Even if Arbat could have kept Gonrod from reporting back, the news of Visser Three's death would have traveled swiftly enough.

A War Council that either needed to deny, or did not even know of a mission to Earth, would have found an announcement of success a bit of an embarrassment.

Then the deeper truth struck me. <It was about me. You needed me. Only I could give you the location of the Yeerk pool. It is too well shielded from your sensors. You needed me.>

Estrid met my gaze. If she was ashamed she hid it well.

<Your appearance at the newspaper was no accident. You needed to encounter me. And the attack on the Community Center? Necessary to show me that the only remaining alternative was the Yeerk pool — the best place to introduce the virus. You used me.>

<Visser Three murdered your brother. We knew you would have no alternative but to help us kill him.>

I wanted to deny it. Wanted her to deny it. An immoral, illegal, despicable mission, and I was a necessary part of it all. I was a pawn in a terrifying replay of the crimes on the Hork-Bajir world.

Alloran, the Andalite who later became the host body of Visser Three, had directed the use of biologicals to exterminate the Hork-Bajir.

Better dead than hosts and weapons of the Yeerks.

How many Hork-Bajir had died, no one knew. Enough survived to supply shock troops to the Yeerks.

It was a crime that seared the conscience of all Andalites. It was an evil so profound that we would never be free of its taint.

And now, again? Again?

<You cannot do this,> I told Estrid.

<Why not?> She lifted her chin. <I am working to eliminate the instability. But even if it does prove fatal to humans as well as Yeerks, our aims are achieved. The Yeerks will never be able to use this planet as a host colony. The humans will not die in vain. The Yeerk scourge will stop here. They will not succeed in enslaving one more race.>

<Your logic is indisputable. Yet, if the price of freedom is the loss of an entire sentient species, then perhaps the price is too high.>

<The universe is a vast place, Aximili-Esgarrouth-Isthill. We cannot afford to be senti-

mental about one species. There is too much at stake.

<Aximili, if you only understood the elegance of the equations. If you could grasp the mathematical beauty. . . . We are on the verge of deploying a weapon that, once it is perfected, will make us invulnerable! We will have absolute power throughout the galaxy! We can destroy the Yeerks. But not only the Yeerks. We can stop all wars, all destruction, annihilate all enemies of decency and goodness before they can carry out their evil!>

<Estrid, if you are prepared to kill everyone, anyone that opposes you,> I asked her, <how are you different from the Yeerks?>

<We are Andalites!>

<Estrid, you cannot do this.>

<Yes, she can,> said a voice in the doorway. <And she will.>

CHAPTER 24

Arbat stood in the doorway, holding a shredder on us.

<I have relieved Gonrod of command,> Arbat answered. <He is confined to his quarters.>

I said, <Arbat, have you told Estrid that her name, her presence here on this ship, her very existence, has already been wiped from the data banks?>

That caught Arbat by surprise. <How —> But he caught himself quickly. <A security precaution.>

<No. Preparation for a suicide mission.> I turned my face to Estrid. <You may imagine that this terrible deed is approved of by the people. But it is not. The Andalite people would arrest

you and charge you as a criminal. That is why the people will never be told. It is why only the dregs of the Andalite military — Aloth and Gonrod — could be used.>

<You have said enough, *Aristh*,> Arbat snarled.

<They needed you, Estrid. They needed a person of your genius to manage the "weapon." But you, like Aloth and Gonrod, will never survive. Arbat cannot allow it. Only he can survive. The Apex Level Intelligence agent who passed himself off as a professor. Why? To find someone like you, Estrid.>

Estrid focused her main eyes on Arbat. <Is it true what Aximili says?> she asked.

Arbat glared at us both, but then his face softened when he looked at Estrid. <Yes. I am truly sorry. I have deceived you. If it is any comfort, it was to protect you.>

<Protect me? From what? You brought me here to die.>

<To protect you from history's judgment,> he said, his voice thick with emotion. <The people must be led by the few who are willing to make the very hard choices. The people are happy in their ignorance. But we in the Apex Level cannot allow ourselves to be sentimental.>

He pressed a button. A control panel slid from the wall. Arbat quickly programmed it.

Bright green streaks shot from floor to ceiling, creating bars. A laser cage around the two of us.

Arbat took the vial from the counter. <I am sorry. You will die, Estrid. But not in vain.>

<Arbat! It is not too late. Do not do it,> I begged.

To my surprise his old, world-weary eyes shone with emotion. <This war must end, *Aristh*. It has caused too much suffering. Too much killing. Think of all the bright young scientists, artists, and thinkers conscripted year after year to feed this war. So many brilliant and creative minds turned from decent pursuits to the job of killing. Good Andalites all. Good Andalites forced to make hard, cruel decisions.>

I would have liked to tail-whip him. None of this was about the Yeerks, the humans, or even the Andalites. It was about what he saw as his duty. His right. The self-pity of the murderer.

<This is not the way to end it,> I told him.

He shook his head. <That is not for you to decide. The strong must decide. The weak can only obey.>

Arbat turned and galloped from the lab.

Estrid tried to follow.

ZZZZZZZ!

The green laser bars erupted in a shower of sparks when Estrid made contact. She was knocked to the floor.

I leaned down. <Estrid!>

<I am fine.>

I helped her to her feet.

<I am sorry, Aximili.>

<It is not your fault.>

<It is. I betrayed you. And your human friends. I have been a fool. A criminal fool. Arbat convinced me that humans were not worth the loss of more galactic life. Unwilling to carry their weight in the fight for freedom. Eager to give up.>

She took my hands. <I did not tell Arbat about your friends. But I did not have to. He was in the barn, too. In a bird morph.>

<Yes, I know,> I answered.

Her stalk eyes whipped around in amazement. <You knew?>

I nodded. <We all knew. Or at least, suspected.>

Marco walked calmly into view. "Hey, Axman. You're looking slightly trapped."

<Where are the others?>

Marco made a sweeping gesture encompassing the lab. "We're here. The place is crawling with Animorphs. Literally."

In various places human forms were growing up out of tiny points. Flea morph. Fly morph. Roach morph.

Cassie and Rachel and Prince Jake.

One morphing mass emerged as a bird rather than a human.

<The bird with the red tail,> Estrid said.

<Tobias. You met him. They all came aboard with me this afternoon. They have used my quarters to demorph and remorph as necessary.>

Tobias ruffled his wings. <Hey, Ax.>

"Go, Tobias, stay on him," Prince Jake said.

<Later, everyone. The Animorph Air Force has a mission.>

Tobias flew out of the room and caught the breeze of the drop shaft.

Estrid looked at me, half amazed, half angry. <It was all a deception. You misled us. You lied to your own people.>

I shook my head. <No. I have learned something, Estrid. These *are* my people. Anyone who believes in freedom, anyone who resists tyranny, anyone who pursues peace is "my people." Andalite, Hork-Bajir, or human.>

"Yeah," Marco said. "Besides, we humans make a mean cinnamon bun."

I laughed. <That is definitely true.>

CHAPTER 25

We flew to the Community Center. It would be Arbat's most likely path into the Yeerk pool. But, unfortunately, it was only an educated guess. Tobias had been unable to follow him. Arbat, ever the intelligence professional, had morphed to human and entered a train station.

Whether he had emerged, or in what shape, we could not tell.

However we were soon certain of which way he had gone.

It was very late at night but the Yeerks still kept up a guard. We found the first human-Controller lying sprawled by the trash. Another slumped in the doorway. A third lay facedown in the hallway.

My human friends were in battle morph. Estrid and I had demorphed to Andalite. Tobias was somewhere outside, flying above, watching. No doubt berating himself unnecessarily for having lost Arbat.

<Tobias?> I called in private thought-speak.

<Yeah, Ax-man?>

<He is here.>

We walked softly through the dark and empty Community Center. Maybe Arbat had eliminated all Yeerk security. Maybe not.

<What are we looking for?> Jake asked me.

<This.> I stopped in front of a door with a sign that said ORIENTATION ROOM. NEW MEMBERS ONLY. <This is where the ship's sensors showed a possible deep hole.>

I looked at the door. There was a lock. But it had been broken. <Arbat,> I said. <He may not be in Andalite form. He may well be human.>

Marco pushed the door open. A dark and seemingly endless staircase yawned before us. <Basement?>

Cassie said, <No. I can hear screams. I know that sound.>

Cassie's wolf morph is possessed of incredibly acute hearing and sense of smell.

<Yeah. I was afraid of that,> Marco said. <You know, I keep saying I'm never, ever going back down there.>

<Say it again,> Rachel said. <Maybe it'll make you feel better.>

<I am never, ever going down there again.>

<Ticktock, people,> Prince Jake said. <We want to get Arbat before he reaches the pool. Let's move.>

We ran down the stairs. Level after level. Tiger pads and bear paws and Andalite hooves all rushing, tripping, rushing again.

As we descended, the sounds of the Yeerk pool — the screams, the cries, the rumble of equipment, became loud enough for Andalite senses to hear.

Estrid said, <Aximili, I am afraid.>

<So am I.>

Down. Faster and faster. Down.

Suddenly I slipped. Fell. Rolled down several steps.

The smell was awful. Part of the staircase was wet with slimy pool water. Gore. Chunks of flesh, piles of quivering entrails. Evidence of a recent Taxxon feeding frenzy.

I jumped up, wiped the gore from my flanks. I tried not to think of it. Tried to focus on what mattered. Arbat had to be stopped. No time to think of the filth, no time to imagine the horror . . .

Ahead the stairs emerged from the ground

into the vast openness of the Yeerk pool complex. After this point we would be visible to anyone looking up from below.

<No Arbat,> Rachel said.

<He's down there,> Prince Jake said. <No choice. We have to go after him. Demorph. It's the only way. Ax and Estrid? I think a pair of Andalites might be a little conspicuous.>

I began to morph to human. Estrid did the same. The Yeerk pool complex would contain humans, Hork-Bajir, Gedds, and Taxxons. But only humans would be expected to come down this particular stairway at this time of night.

"What natural weapons do these humans' bodies have?" Estrid asked.

"Unless you've eaten a lot of beans, none," Marco said.

"Keep your heads down, don't make eye contact," Jake instructed. "We don't want to be ID'd. Don't move fast or seem to be looking around. Now, go!"

We walked down the stairs again. On only two legs.

We could see the pool now. Hork-Bajir and human guards stood watch as other Hork-Bajir and human-Controllers filed down the two steel piers that traversed the main part of the leaden pool. Each pier was lined with locking collars.

As guards supervised, the Controllers kneeled down and placed their necks in metal collars.

When the collars snapped into place, a small gray slug crawled out of the Controller's ear and fell into the dank pool with a soft plop!

The hosts were then momentarily free. Free at least to control their own mouths and eyes. They could cry. They did. They could beg. They did that, too.

"This is obscene," Estrid whispered fiercely.

"Pretend to be unconcerned," I said.

"Spread out," Prince Jake muttered as we merged with a group of human-Controllers.

Estrid and I stayed close, but drifted from the others. Human-Controllers everywhere. Some jocular as they hooked up with Yeerk friends. Most just businesslike. They were here to feed, not socialize.

Faces everywhere. Hundreds. Which was Arbat? Impossible to say. Impossible to guess where he would be in this . . .

No. Not impossible. He would pursue his mission as swiftly as possible. He would deliver the virus into the pool.

The pier. Of course.

But how to spot him? He would look human. Would *be* human. Just like all these human-Controllers.

No. Not like them. The Controllers all had access to human experience, human knowledge. A human morph is only instinct. Harder to control, harder to understand easily. As I knew from experience.

I tried to think. Time was running out. Arbat might already have struck. How to spot an Andalite in human morph?

What was different? Two legs, not four. No tail. Two eyes, not four.

"Estrid! Look for humans who turn their heads frequently."

"What?"

"We are accustomed to seeing in all directions at once. Humans are used to not knowing what is behind them. Look for —"

I froze. A middle-aged man. Walking down the length of the crowded pier, escorted by a nonchalant Hork-Bajir.

The man turned as a Taxxon passed behind him. Turned again. Turned.

No proof. Not enough to be sure. A feeling . . .

"There!" I started to run toward the pier. Estrid raced alongside me.

<Jake!> I cried out in private thought-speak. <He's a middle-aged lightly colored male human. On the pier!>

"Must be late for a feeding," a Controller laughed as I brushed past him.

The middle-aged man knelt. Placed his

head into the collar beside a kneeling Hork-Bajir.

The Hork-Bajir guard leaned down to fasten the collar. The man reached into his pocket.

Too far away!

"Arbat! No!" Estrid yelled.

The man jerked his head up. His movement was quick and unexpected. The Hork-Bajir guard was knocked off balance, teetered almost comically.

Arbat reached to grab the Hork-Bajir. Or so the Hork-Bajir thought. Arbat grabbed the guard's Dracon beam from his holster with one hand and shoved the off balance Hork-Bajir off the pier.

Arbat spun, raised his weapon, and aimed.

CHAPTER 26

I dove forward. Tackled Estrid. We fell behind a large, lumbering Taxxon.

Arbat fired.

Tseeewww!

The bloated Taxxon broke open. The foul contents of its stomach spewed in every direction. Blood. Bile. Entrails.

<Battle morphs!> I heard Prince Jake yell. Faraway or near, I could not tell.

"Estrid!" I dragged her to her feet, slipping in the gore.

Another Taxxon was rushing in our direction, eager to eat what was left of his former comrade.

Hork-Bajir guards, pounded along the steel pier, trying to locate the source of the trouble.

There was chaos but in seconds the Hork-Bajir might restore order.

Then Estrid and I would be dead.

"Andalites! Andalites!" I shouted. I yelled and waved my hands, pointing always down the pier. "Andalite bandits in Hork-Bajir morph! The Hork-Bajir are Andalites!"

Estrid joined in. "Help! Help! Security! Andalites have morphed the Hork-Bajir!"

Chaos would reign a while longer.

But Arbat, too, took advantage of the confusion. I spotted him running.

<He is heading toward the cage area!> I yelled.

<I see him! I'm on him!> Rachel yelled back.

I had lost sight of Arbat. And I could not see Rachel. But I got a grim satisfaction from the thought of what the intelligence agent slash professor would see when next he turned around to look.

Estrid and I lurched, slipping and sliding, off the pier. Back onto packed dirt. We shoved our way through the crush of human-Controllers.

"Cowards!" someone yelled at us.

Then, <I lost him!> Rachel yelled in frustration. <Past the cages.>

I had to get Arbat. He could demorph, remorph, and we would lose him permanently. And possibly lose much of the human species.

I yanked Estrid around behind a large wooden crate, pulled her down, dragged her after me as I crawled into the space between the crate and the side of the human-Controllers' cafeteria.

"Estrid, demorph!"

"They will kill us!" She was frightened. Frightened deep down inside. Frightened in a way that was erasing any thought but the screaming, desperate need to live.

I knew the feeling.

"We have to stop Arbat and we need firepower," I said.

"Why? To save these filthy Yeerks? Look what they do. Look at what they are! They are going to do that to us, Aximili! They will drag us down that pier, they will force us . . . NO! Kill them all!"

"Estrid, you said the virus may mutate. You said it might affect humans as well."

"Might. Maybe. But maybe I fixed it. Maybe my last adjustments eliminated the random flux. I do not care! They are not our people. I am not going to let the filthy slugs do that to me!"

I was half demorphed. <Stay here,> I said. <Stay low, do not move.>

"Do not leave me!"

<Estrid, you are beautiful, you are brilliant. But I really do not think I like you very much.>

I took a deep breath. Tried to steady my nerves. Impossible.

I leaped out.

Fwapp! Hit a Hork-Bajir.

The cages. The nearest was a hundred feet away.

"Andalite!" a human-Controller screamed in my face.

<Correct,> I said and knocked him down.

I ran for the cages.

Pandemonium! Dracon fire from three different locations. Screams. Shouts. The roar of furious Hork-Bajir. The slithery squeaks of ravenous Taxxons.

I ran.

Tseeew!

The shot missed, the human-Controller had been in too much of a hurry.

Fwapp! Now he could take his time.

A Taxxon blocked my way. I leaped.

Ahead, a battle. A tiger, a wolf, a bear, a gorilla, surrounded, backs against a row of cages. Marco held a middle-aged human by the neck with one hand and fought with the other hand.

Their backs were to the cages. It would have been child's play for the Yeerks to simply shoot them through the bars. Shoot them in the back.

But the human hosts in that cage, slaves of the Yeerks temporarily free of those Yeerks, stood there, arms linked, blocking the shot. A human shield.

The Hork-Bajir could have burned them down. Those humans knew that. They were putting themselves between the supposed Andalites and the Yeerks, ready to face Dracon fire.

The Hork-Bajir had no orders to massacre hosts. Visser Three was not in the pool. No one else would dare give the order.

I attacked the force that hemmed in my friends. Struck left and right, took them by surprise. But all for nothing. We could fight, but we could not win.

I saw Cassie knocked unconscious.

Saw Prince Jake slashing with one paw, the other front paw gone, a stump.

Tseeew!

A beam caught Marco full in the belly. A hole appeared in his rough black fur. He fell. Released his grip on Arbat.

Arbat ran. No one stopped him. Why would they? He was a human-Controller being held by the Andalites.

He ran, pushed through the attackers. Ran toward the reinfestation pier. I saw the green vial in his hand.

<Prince Jake! Arbat . . .>

<Go!> Prince Jake said.

I hesitated. How could I leave my friends? They were dying.

I turned, ran, raced after Arbat.

He made the pier. No one guarded it. All the Hork-Bajir had gone to the fight. Three Taxxons shuffled along its length. Voluntary hosts awaiting reinfestation.

Arbat raced to the end of the pier. He was panting, wheezing. The middle-aged human morph was not athletic.

He fumbled, hastening to open the vial.

<Arbat!> I yelled.

"You!"

One of the Taxxons noticed us at last. The red jelly eyes jiggled. But I was not concerned with the Taxxon. No Taxxon would attack an Andalite.

<Do not do it, Arbat.>

"You are very fast, *Aristh* Aximili. But you are not fast enough to cover fifty feet before I can open my fist."

<It is wrong, Arbat.>

"It is war, *Aristh* Aximili."

He smiled at me. And he began to open his hand.

CHAPTER 27

<No!>

Tseeew!

The beam passed so close to me that I felt it singe my stalk eyes.

The beam hit Arbat's human hand.

The hand, and the vial it held, sizzled and burned and disappeared in a wisp of smoke.

I turned one stalk eye back to see Estrid. She lowered the Dracon beam.

<Good shot,> I said.

<Yes. I suppose it was.>

Blood pumped from Arbat's stump. It didn't matter. Arbat had only to demorph to end the pain of the wound.

<It is all over, Arbat.>

<Now what?> Estrid asked me.

I nodded toward the shore where part of the force besieging my friends peeled off to come roaring after us.

<Now we die,> I said. <But we die as honorable Andalite warriors.>

<Do not let them take me alive,> Estrid said to me. <Even if you do not approve of me, Aximili.>

A wave of Hork-Bajir rushed at us. I braced for the attack. Estrid beside me.

Arbat chose not to join us.

"Andalites!" he screamed, pointing at us with his remaining hand. "Andalites! Look what they did to me!"

And then the Yeerk pool just to our left began to boil. There was a red circle, fifty feet in diameter, projected on the roiling liquid and everything within that circle was boiling, steaming, hissing.

I stared, transfixed. Estrid, always the physicist, saw what I had missed.

<No, up! Up there!>

I raised my main eyes to the domed roof of the Yeerk pool. There, at the highest point, a hole! Stars! I saw stars!

The red beam stopped suddenly. The wide-angle shredder beam on the *Ralek River* must have taken five minutes to slowly burn its way through the earthen dome.

<It can't be done,> I whispered, not daring to hope.

Through the hole, into the Yeerk pool flew the old ship, the tired, out-of-date relic named the *Ralek River.*

TSEEEW! TSEEEW!

The ship's shredders would never be a match for Bug fighters let alone the Blade ship, but they were more than enough to stop the onrushing Hork-Bajir.

Ten feet of pier between us and the Yeerks sizzled and evaporated.

TSEEEW! TSEEEW!

A line of destruction burned between the half-dead Animorphs and their attackers.

The ship flew low and slow, hovered directly above us.

Tseew! Tseeew! Hork-Bajir were firing back with handheld Dracon weapons. Like trying to kill an elephant by throwing rocks.

A ramp lowered. I pushed Estrid toward it and leaped aboard myself.

"Wait!" Arbat yelled.

I hesitated.

"I am an Andalite, too! I am one of your own people!"

He reached up toward me with his one human hand and his one bloody stump.

<Go,> I told Gonrod.

The ship lifted and slid toward the cages.

If Arbat had thought to demorph instantly he might have lived a while longer. He stood there, raging, trapped on a segment of pier, alone.

Alone but for the Taxxons whose eternal hunger would not let them ignore the smell of his blood.

CHAPTER 28

Rachel and Cassie went to the mall to buy Estrid a cinnamon bun. I gave it to her as a going-away present. Told her to enjoy it on the long trip home to Andalite space.

Gonrod had flown the ship back to its berth beside The Gardens. It made sense. After the daring assault on the Yeerk pool, every Yeerk ship in Earth space was on high alert. A day spent waiting would make escape easier.

It might have been no great loss if the *Ralek River* were destroyed, but a pilot like Gonrod, insufferable as he might be, was a treasure.

<Is this as delicious as the jelly beans?> Estrid asked, holding the warm paper box.

<Even more,> I said.

<And this is why you care for these humans?>

I thought of the human hosts who had made a shield of their bodies to protect my friends. Thought of the many, many, uncountable times Prince Jake or Rachel or Cassie or Marco or Tobias had risked death to help me.

<Yes,> I said. <That is why I like humans. It is all about the cinnamon buns.>

<Aximili, come home with me. Together, the two of us and Gonrod, we can make the people realize the truth.>

I shook my head. <My fight is here,> I said.

<Is it because you still do not like me?> She tried for a lighthearted tone.

I nodded. <I still do not like you,> I said.

I left the ship. Walked away from my chance to be home again. I rejoined my friends.

The *Ralek River* took off. Did it escape Visser Three's dragnet? Did it make it safely into Zero-space?

I do not know.

I walked away and did not look back.

I morphed to human as we six walked together. Even Tobias became human, I think to be near me, to "hang" as the humans say.

Cassie put her arm around my shoulder. It is a human gesture of comfort. "You okay?" she asked.

"Why wouldn't he be?" Marco said. "You heard him. He didn't even like her."

Cassie said nothing but squeezed me a bit tighter. Cassie is not easily deceived.

"Let's get something to eat, man, I'm starved," Rachel said.

"Anything but McDonald's," Tobias said.

"What, the mouse hunter is getting picky about burgers?" Marco said.

"No, that's not it."

Prince Jake raised an eyebrow. "Tobias? Is there something you need to tell me?"

Tobias shrugged. "Well, you know, I saw Yeerk reinforcements pouring into the Community Center so I knew you guys were in trouble, right?"

"Right. So you went for Gonrod."

"Exactly. I asked him if we could burn through into the Yeerk pool. He said, "Maybe, but only at the thinnest point." Anyway, late as it was, even the night cleanup crew was gone . . ."

"No," Prince Jake said. "You didn't. You did not obliterate a McDonald's."

"Like it was never there," Tobias said with a laugh. "The Yeerks will fill the hole before anyone realizes what's down there underneath the ground, but if we want burgers, I'm thinking Burger King."

"I would like a burger," I said. "Burrr-ger."

We walked along the dark streets, my friends and I. My more-than-friends. We laughed, so relieved to simply be alive. We joked.

Cassie held my hand, and in the darkness where no one could see, I cried.

Don't miss

#39 The Hidden

I crashed through the underbrush, trampling saplings and ripping through sticker bushes without a second thought.

The scent of the real Cape buffalo was thick in my nostrils. I followed it deeper and deeper into the woods until the screams and shouts of the Controllers back at the roadblock were completely lost.

The buffalo's hearing — my hearing now — absorbed and gauged every sound, checking for any potential threat to my herd.

My depth perception wasn't so great but I had a three-hundred-and-sixty degree wide-angle range of vision, which was going to make it pretty rough for anyone to sneak up on me.

This was a good thing.

I couldn't run very fast — nowhere near the speed of my wolf morph — but what the buffalo lacked in miles per hour, it definitely made up for in sheer bulk and muscle. Nobody, and I mean *nobody* — except maybe a lion — would take me on, and I could still outrun a lion if I had to.

And then there was man. The most infuriating scent, the most unnatural threat.

But the air was clean of man-scent.

The buffalo's brain, so powerful in its fury, began to shift its concentration in the quiet woods. Sort of downgraded from an all-out, fight-to-the-death attack mode to a standby alert that noted all sight, scents, and sounds, then dismissed them as nonthreatening.

It was a relief. It allowed me to get a firmer grip on the buffalo's natural instincts.

<Okay, Cassie, I told Jake you got away and you're all clear to demorph,> Tobias said, wheeling high in the sky above me. <The helicopters are still back over The Gardens trying to track down the others. Chapman got up but they loaded him into an ambulance. The Controllers are going nuts because they had to call in a whole fleet of tow trucks and Visser Three's limo's a total disaster.>

<Yeah, I guess my buffalo buddy and I got a little carried away,> I said, kind of embarrassed.

I found a dense bramble thicket where I could demorph, then thinking twice, moved on until I was in a small clearing surrounded by a few trees. The thorns and stickers might not have hurt the buffalo's tough hide but they would've ripped my skin to shreds.

<Tobias, has anyone come up with a plan for destroying the Helmacron ship's sensors, yet?>

<No, but we're going to have to figure out something fast. Definitely before those helicopters decide to change their focus and come after the box again.> Tobias swooped down and landed on a nearby branch.

I opened my mouth and dropped the slippery, spit-covered box on the ground. Then focused on my own DNA and felt the changes begin.

Even though everyone says I have a talent for morphing — and I have to admit I usually can sort of control the process — it still doesn't follow any real, precise pattern. So I wasn't surprised when the first thing to go this time was my tail. It drooped slowly and then started to melt like hot wax, then —

SCHLOOP!

Was sucked right back up into my body.

Bones began to grind and crunch, reshaping themselves.

My eyes crawled closer together. My ears shriveled and shrank.

SPROOT! SPROOT!

Ten human toes shot out of the crumbling hooves. My bones adjusted and reformed into ankles, then knees, then hips. My massive horns crumpled, deflated, and rolled back up toward the cleft at the center of my head.

<Yuck,> Tobias said, ruffling his feathers and looking the other way. <No offense, Cassie, but that is really gross. I'm glad I haven't eaten anything in a while.>

I began to say, "I know," but it came out as, "Waaaw waaw."

"I know," I repeated, once my jaw finished shrinking. I flexed my fingers, bent down, and picked up the box. "And I know something else, too. We might want to steer clear of the real buffalo if we can. I, uh, don't think it trusts humans very much."

<No problem,> Tobias said. <The last time I saw it was about a mile ahead of you and still running.>

"Good," I said, exhaling. "The Gardens'll send out a search party and probably a helicopter . . ."

Oh, that was a nice picture. And just what we didn't need. My mother buzzing around the sky, searching for a lost Cape buffalo, while we dodged Yeerks in helicopters who were trying to kill us.

Tobias cocked his head. Listening. <Uh-oh.>

"What?"

<Tell you in a minute,> he said. I watched him lift off, make a quick circle. <Helicopter, Cassie. The Yeerks are expanding their search. We'd better get going.>

<You Can Run But You Can't Hide>

ANIMORPHS

K. A. Applegate

The pint-sized Helmacrons have departed Earth, but left a morph-tracking system behind. Now the Yeerks have found it and are prepared to launch a full-blown hunt for the Animorphs. Armed with their dangerous new weapon, nothing can stop the Yeerks from tracking down their foes.

What can save the Animorphs now?

ANIMORPHS #39: THE HIDDEN

Visit the Web site at: http://www.scholastic.com/animorphs